Savannah's

Amish Ties That Bind

THE AMISH WOMEN OF
LAWRENCE COUNTY SERIES - BOOK 6

Tracy Fredrychowski

ISBN: 979-8-9879040-9-1 (paperback)

ISBN: 979-8-9906105-7-6 (large print)

ISBN: 979-8-9879040-8-4 (digital)

Copyright © 2024 by Tracy Fredrychowski

Cover Design by Tracy Lynn Virtual, LLC

Cover Background Photograph by Jim Fisher

Published in South Carolina by The Tracer Group, LLC

https://tracyfredrychowski.com

i

Tracy Fredrychowski

To my granddaughter, Hailey Mae.

Your strength and spirited nature have brought warmth and

joy to my world from the moment I first saw you.

By Tracy Fredrychowski

AMISH OF LAWRENCE COUNTY SERIES

Secrets of Willow Springs – Book 1

Secrets of Willow Springs – Book 2

Secrets of Willow Springs – Book 3

APPLE BLOSSOM INN SERIES

Love Blooms at the Apple Blossom Inn

An Amish Christmas at the Apple Blossom Inn

NOVELLA'S

The Amish Women of Lawrence County

An Amish Gift Worth Waiting For

The Orphans' Amish Christmas

THE AMISH WOMEN OF LAWRENCE COUNTY

Emma's Amish Faith Tested – Book 1

Rebecca's Amish Heart Restored – Book 2

Anna's Amish Fears Revealed – Book 3

Barbara's Amish Truth Exposed – Book 4

Allie's Amish Family Miracle – Book 5

Savannah's Amish Ties That Bind – Book 6

A WILLOW SPRINGS MYSTERY ROMANCE

The Amish Book Cellar – Book 1

www.tracyfredrychowski.com

Contents

A NOTE ABOUT AMISH VOCABULARY

The Amish language is called Pennsylvania Dutch and is usually spoken rather than written. The spelling of commonly used words varies from community to community throughout the United States and Canada. Even as I researched this book, some words' spelling changed within the same Amish community that inspired this story. In one case, spellings were debated between family members. Some of the terms may have slightly different spellings. Still, all came from my interactions with the Amish settlement near where I was raised in northwestern Pennsylvania.

While this book was modeled upon a small community in Lawrence County, this is a work of fiction. The names and characters are products of my imagination. They do not resemble any person, living or dead, or actual events in that community.

LIST OF CHARACTERS

Savannah Carmicheal. A twenty-four-year-old event management executive from Charleston, Savannah, is known for her feisty personality. Embarking on a journey of self-discovery, she seeks to discover who she truly wants to become.

Neal Zook. For six years, his past mistakes have held him captive. His journey involves seeking redemption and finding peace.

Gigi. Savannah's grandmother lives and is filled with faith. Gigi's wisdom and gentle guidance are crucial to Savannah's journey.

Harold and Priscilla Zook. Neal's Amish parents. Their sound advice and gentle ways guide Savannah and Neal on their paths to redemption.

David Zook. Neal's younger brother, who is not pleased with Neal's return to Willow Springs and harbors resentment.

Rosalie Mast. Neal's childhood sweetheart, who challenges Savannah to swallow her pride and learn to handle conflict in a Christian manner.

Sarah Byler. Savannah's best friend in Willow Springs offers support and guidance as she navigates her new life.

Bishop Weaver. The district bishop of the Old Order Amish community provides spiritual guidance and leadership.

Bishop Schrock. The district bishop of the New Order Fellowship offers a more modern perspective while maintaining Amish values.

MAP OF WILLOW SPRINGS

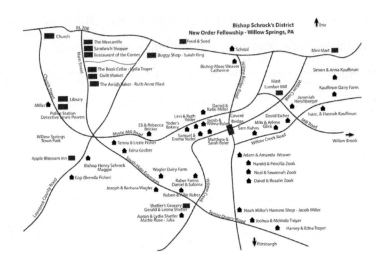

PROLOGUE
Charleston, South Carolina

I remember the day I first laid eyes on Neal Carmichael. I'd been trying to maneuver a large box up three flights of stairs when he took it from my hands and delivered it to my third-floor apartment, taking the steps two at a time.

Over the next few weeks, I watched him from my upstairs window like clockwork. Twice a day, he would carry his bike outside and disappear into Charleston, South Carolina's busy cobblestone streets. I never knew where he went, but I held my breath until he returned.

There was something different about him—something about the way he carried himself. It suggested there was more to him than what met the eye. And what met the eye was quite

1

appealing. Aside from his chestnut brown hair, which he kept perfectly shaped, and his wide-set eyes that were speckled with hints of green, I only knew he lived on the first floor and rode his bike everywhere he went and didn't own a car as far as I could tell.

He had the sweetest accent. On the rare occasion he spoke or at least acknowledged my existence, his tone carried a gentle lilt, each syllable pronounced with care, as if speaking English wasn't his first language. When I questioned his nationality, his eyes expressed aloofness as he replied, "American."

Confused and lost in the melodic cadence of his words, I tucked his response away and inquired about the weather instead. "Is it always this hot in April?"

He swung a long leg over his tapered bicycle and waved as he took off down the street, replying to my question. "Wouldn't know. Only been here a few months."

With temperatures already hovering near eighty degrees, I watched him become a fading figure in the Charleston landscape. I could still feel the breeze that carried the perfume from the Carolina Jessamine outside our apartment building that morning. Had I known the pain I would have endured by pursuing him, I would have walked away that balmy spring morning, never to look back.

And I, Savannah Carmichael, now an unemployed event management executive, was packing boxes in my posh Ashley River condo without knowing where my husband was or if he was ever coming home. I had no choice but to return to my grandmother's Willow Springs, Pennsylvania, home. The home—and I use the word loosely—had been left to her by my grandfather, and its upkeep had been mainly ignored.

I often spoke to my grandmother but ignored her invitations to visit on more than one occasion. Her eccentric manner and simple living tendencies went against the high-living expectations I had for my life.

I cherished my summer visits with my Gigi (as she liked to be called), as I was often sent there to stay when my parents wanted a reprieve from my constant chatter. Even though we lived on the shores of Lake Erie, less than an hour away, my parents rarely visited her for long.

While I knew my grandmother loved me, and I could always count on her to give me sound advice, especially after the relationship with my parents became nonexistent, there was something mysterious about her. Something I could never quite place. She enjoyed life like no one I'd ever known. Even after Poppy passed, she found joy in the simplest things. Mom said it was because she spent too much time with her Amish neighbors. But Dad said she kept her nose buried in the Bible so much she lost all sense of the real world.

Regardless, all I have to look forward to now is a run-down house on the edge of an Amish town with a peculiar grandmother with whom I don't have anything in common.

And now, after the disturbing realization that my husband of five years has come up missing with no traceable explanation, along with my dream job, I'm forced to leave this beautiful city behind. It wasn't how I had planned to spend my morning, let alone my life.

CHAPTER 1

One Month Earlier – Charleston, South Carolina

S avannah leaned against the cool railing of her balcony. The southern sun had yet to warm its iron, and she welcomed the feel against her skin. She gazed over the picturesque scenes of the Ashley River as it meandered through Charleston. The early autumn air had a hint of crispness, tinged with the salty harbor. The historical city was coming to life; the huge oaks lining the streets were swaying, bringing a momentary breeze to the cobblestone streets.

Her condo, a blend of modern and southern charm, perched high above the arts district, was the perfect retreat from her demanding career as an event planner at Belle Haven Celebrations, one of Charleston's premier event management firms.

Sipping on her favorite French vanilla latte, she couldn't help but take in the rich aroma as she reflected on her life. It was nearly perfect. She was at the peak of her career, working with some of the South's most influential families. It was more than a job; it was a passion that consumed much of her time and energy.

Besides her career, Neal was her handsome and sometimes mysterious husband, her steadfast supporter. He was a constant source of strength and put up with her long hours with such grace that she couldn't imagine how any other man would put up with both her ever-changing moods and sassy personality.

Savannah's quick decision-making skills made her popular among her clients, but they often spilled over into her personal life, where she found herself hard-pressed to adapt to compromise in married life. Neal often likened her to 'a feral barn cat,' with her fiery independence and occasional temper flare-ups.

Yet, as she watched a lone sailboat gliding across the river, a nagging feeling tugged at her heart. Despite the overwhelming sense of contentment, there was a subtle whisper in the back of her mind that something was amiss with her husband. He'd been distracted lately; his usual attentive manner was replaced with something she couldn't quite place. Was it stress from his job or something more? There was an edge about him that she'd never witnessed before, which left her unsettled. But she shook it off then, hoping it was just a residual effect of her busy season.

Taking the last sip from her mug, she headed inside with thoughts about the new campaign she was about to pitch to her team that morning. It was an idea that could elevate her career even further. She needed to focus... to bring her best to the table that morning. "It's just pre-presentation nerves," she murmured as she entered the kitchen.

Neal was already up, dressed in his usual business attire, looking every bit the successful executive as he prepared their breakfast. The smell of avocado toast, her favorite, filled the air as she greeted him with a quick kiss on the cheek.

"You're the greatest. How did I get so lucky?" she whispered as she hugged him. He didn't answer as he handed her a plate and motioned her toward the breakfast bar. "Big day today, huh?"

"The biggest," Savannah replied as she took a bite.

"Anything else you need?" he asked, his smile not quite reaching his eyes. She thought he seemed a tad too eager to please, almost forced for some reason.

Savannah watched his movements as he wiped down the countertop. She wanted to question him, but the clock reminded her of her tight schedule. She grabbed her keys and purse off the counter and stopped before opening the door. "Stir-fry for dinner?"

Neal scrunched up his nose at her request. "If that's what you want."

Chinese wasn't his favorite, but the takeout restaurant was on her way home and would make for a quick dinner. "We'll figure something out later," she promised as she headed out the door. Little did she know that the later wouldn't be the one she anticipated, and her perfect little life was soon about to show its hidden cracks.

***

Savannah's heels clicked against the polished marble floor of the hallway of Belle Haven Celebrations expansive office. The rising Charleston sun flowed in through the floor-to-ceiling windows of the old historic building as she strode into the conference room. Her stomach fluttered excitedly as she prepared to reveal her plan to propel her company's position.

"All right, everyone," she commanded her team's attention. "Today, we redefine weddings with 'Legacy of Love'—a campaign that combines luxury with tradition, leveraging Charleston's historic charm to offer the most elegant wedding experiences on the East Coast."

Her team focused on the screen behind her as she clicked the remote, bringing her presentation to life. Images of Charleston's landscape blended with scenes of potential wedding setups: elegant receptions in antebellum mansions, charming carriage rides, and sunset toasts by the harbor.

The room erupted in applause as she concluded. As the meeting broke up, her assistant, Jenna, said, that's fantastic! It's fresh and bold and will take our wedding events to a whole new level, let alone attract a fresh wave of high-end clients from around the country."

"Thank you, Jenna. Do you want to grab lunch? How about Virginia's on King?" Savannah suggested while checking her phone. She smiled when a message from Neal popped up, a simple heart emoji. "Love you too," she texted back before slipping the phone into her purse.

Lunch at Virginia's was filled with laughter and lighthearted conversation about their weekend plans with a hint of office gossip. Yet, Savannah's phone, now positioned on the table, was buzzing with another Neal message.

"Someone's popular today," Jenna teased, nodding toward the phone.

Savannah laughed it off. "He's been extra sweet today. I think he might be planning something special for the weekend." But down deep, a knot of worry began to grow. He'd been somewhat aloof lately, and this sudden burst of attentiveness left a bitter taste in her mouth... almost as if he was compensating for something.

As the waiter delivered the check, another short text came in about dinner. "Let's skip takeout. I'll cook."

She paused, her initial desire for a quick and easy dinner replaced with Neal's abnormal need to prepare a meal.

The rest of the day passed in a blur of meetings. By the time Savannah made it home, Neal was already in the kitchen, the aroma of roasted chicken filling the air.

"Smells amazing," Savannah said as she dropped her keys and settled at the counter.

Neal turned from the stove, a smile playing on his lips. "Just trying my hand at some good old-fashioned comfort food."

Savannah inhaled the scent of herbs and vegetables neatly arranged in the roasting pan he'd pulled from the oven. The simple, homey dish looked delicious, yet it piqued her curiosity about his past, a topic he didn't like to discuss.

"Is this the type of food you were raised on?" she asked timidly, hoping he'd share even the most minor tidbit about his childhood.

He didn't answer immediately as the question hung in the air for a moment longer than Savannah had hoped. When he finally turned around, his smile was still in place, but his eyes held a guarded stare.

"Somewhat. My mom made chicken every Saturday, and we ate the leftovers Sunday evening. She had an old roasting pan seasoned from years of use. She said it made everything taste better."

"That sounds nice... comforting." Eager to draw more out of him, she pressed on. "Did she use any special seasonings or anything?"

11

She studied him closely and noticed a sudden shift in his composure as he returned to the stove, stirring a flour slurry into the pan drippings for gravy. "Not really. Just simple food, most of which we raised ourselves."

Savannah nodded, sensing he was nearing the edge of his comfort zone on the topic. He was open about his work, interests, and opinions on practically every new gadget on the market. However, the topic of his family or his past was not up for discussion.

She wrapped her arms around his middle as he continued to work at the stove. "Do you think I'll ever get to meet your family?"

He sighed, wiggling free from her backward embrace. "It's complicated," he muttered, pouring the gravy into a small glass pitcher.

Savannah knew not to push further; it would only make him close up even more. Still, she couldn't help but feel that a significant part of his life would always remain a mystery, perhaps too painful or private to revisit.

They moved through their evening routine, discussing a quick trip to Myrtle Beach for the weekend as they tidied up the kitchen. When Neal's phone buzzed, cutting through the usual domestic bliss, he checked the caller ID, and she noticed his face fall.

"I need to take this," he said, stepping onto the balcony.

Savannah watched him through the glass, his facial expression tight. When he returned to the sofa, his mood had noticeably darkened.

"Everything okay?"

"Yeah, just work stuff—nothing to worry about." But as he flipped through the channels, his fidgety knee told another story.

Finally, he stood abruptly. "I need to run to the store. We're out of a few things for breakfast tomorrow."

"At this hour? Can't it wait? I can always grab something at the coffee shop near the office."

Neal insisted, his tone a little too casual for his strange response to the phone call. He leaned down and kissed her, a long, deep kiss that felt more like a goodbye than a see-you-soon. "I love you," he huskily murmured in her ear, then he was gone.

Alone, she flipped off the television and tried to lose herself in a book, but her mind replayed Neal's behavior, his nervousness, the secretive phone call, and his sudden departure.

Something wasn't right. The minutes turned into hours, each minute stretching longer than the last until she fell asleep.

***

Neal's heart sank as his phone buzzed against the coffee table. The screen displayed his boss's name, and with a sense of dread, he stepped outside for privacy. Savannah's gaze followed him, and he tried to give her a reassuring smile before sliding the glass door shut.

"Neal, what on earth's going on?" The voice of his boss, Mr. Evans, was firm and angry as soon as he answered the call. "I just got off the phone with Spencer Tech, our new partners. They've run a preliminary background check on all of our key personnel. Care to explain why there are so many discrepancies in your records?"

Neal felt his heartbeat quicken. He'd hoped to fix things before anyone noticed. "I'm looking into it, sir," he said while trying to keep his voice steady. "There might have been some mistake with the paperwork. I'll take care of it when I return to work."

"A mistake? This isn't just a clerical error, Carmichael!" Mr. Evans's voice grew louder. "They're questioning the authenticity of your credentials, and this is a government contract, so we can't afford any mistakes. What is this all about? They say your transcripts from the technical college you attended have been falsified. Your entire profile has misleading information that makes no sense. This puts your position here at risk, and frankly, the company's reputation too."

Neal's mind raced. He had fabricated parts of his past to escape the life he once knew, to build something new as an *Englischer* far away from his Anabaptist roots. He thought he'd covered all his bases and never imagined it could come crashing down so quickly. "I understand, sir. Give me twenty-four hours, and I'll straighten it out."

"You have until tomorrow morning to give me a good explanation and a clean record, or I'm afraid there will be serious consequences." The line went dead.

Neal stayed on the balcony, the cool night air doing nothing to calm his nerves. He looked in toward Savannah, and she had snuggled down on the couch, looking happy and content with the life they'd built together. With a sinking feeling, he realized there was no easy way out of the mess he had created.

If his actual past came to light, not only was his job at stake, but also the possibility of legal repercussions. Worst of all, it would destroy his trust and love with Savannah. Everything about their life was built on a lie, and he was sure she wouldn't be so quick to forgive his deception... especially after learning about her trauma-filled childhood.

After sitting beside her for a few minutes, he stood and explained his need to run to the store. He kissed her then, a long, tender kiss that was both a goodbye and an apology. Savannah responded by curling her hand around his neck as if she could sense his need for reassurance.

Pulling away, he memorized her face, his love for her stronger than ever. "I love you," he whispered, then turned toward the door before he could change his mind.

Leaning back on the door after closing it, he said a silent goodbye and ran down the two flights of stairs to the street. He knew nothing would ever be the same, but it was the only way to shield her from the coming chaos. With a heavy heart, he started walking, each step away from his home, away from his life, and away from the woman he loved.

***

After leaving the condo, Neal wandered aimlessly through the streets of Charleston until he found himself under the Ravenel Bridge. The only sounds were the distant hum of traffic and the gentle lapping of the water below. Alone on the cold park bench, the city's lights twinkled like distant stars across the water, his mind spun from the events of the evening.

His phone, the bearer of bad news, buzzed in his pocket. Hesitant, he pulled it out to see a message from the man who had crafted his new identity years ago—a man only known to him as "Fletcher."

(Fletcher) *What's up? Saw your missed calls.*

(Neal) *We have a big problem. My background check has issues, and I need your help fixing them.*

(Fletcher) *What kind of problems?*

(Neal) *My educational credentials and SSN are being questioned. They're not matching up with some databases they have.*

(Fletcher) *I did what you paid me for. I gave you a new life. However, I never guaranteed that it would hold up under a forensic-level background check.*

Neal's fingers trembled as he typed, each message sent with a growing sense of urgency.

(Neal) *I need to know exactly what you submitted. They're threatening my job and bringing up criminal charges.*

(Fletcher) *I don't keep records. Safer that way. I can't fix records that weren't legit to begin with.*

(Neal) *So, what am I to do?*

(Fletcher) *Maybe it's time you faced up to who you really are. Can't run from your past forever.*

(Neal) *You promised me a fresh start. I trusted you!*

(Fletcher) *And you got six years out of it. I'm not a miracle worker. You might need to face the music on this one, dude.*

Neal stared at the screen, the words blurring as deep despair settled. Each new text dashed any remaining hope for a simple solution. He was out of options and time and soon out of a job, let alone losing Savannah in the process.

With a heavy sigh, Neal typed a last message.

(Neal) *Thanks for nothing.*

The night grew colder, and Neal wrapped his arms around himself. He thought of returning and confessing everything to Savannah, but the thought of one more person in her life who broke their promises kept him glued to the bench.

In the beginning, he wanted to protect her from his past, from the truth, but now that protection felt more like a wild animal in a cage. He had walked away earlier to protect her from the fallout, but now he wasn't sure if anything was left to protect.

Under the shadow of the massive bridge, with its marshy Charleston breeze swirling around his face, Neal faced the reality that he couldn't truly run from who he really was. The air was thick with the scent of brine and earth, which seemed to carry whispers of his past, immersed in the simple reality of the Amish life he left behind.

As he closed his eyes, his mind drifted to the rolling fields of Northwestern Pennsylvania. The lush green landscape was so different from the busy streets of southern South Carolina.

Before that dreadful night, when his life and the lives of three young boys changed in a matter of hours, he enjoyed the safe haven of a community where hard work and humility gave him a sense of belonging and purpose. Until that point, he'd never dreamed of leaving the security it offered.

With each gust of salty air, the clatter of horse hooves and the rustle of cornfields gave way to the soft murmur of his family's evening prayers. The sounds he left behind still haunted him as reminders of a life dictated by community tradition, not forged by documents and fabricated identities.

He left that quiet existence thinking he could forge a new path without consequence, without the shame that came with bad choices. But now, the fundamentals of that very upbringing, the value of truth and integrity, were the things unraveling his reality.

Leaning back on the bench, he opened his eyes, his stare lifting to the sturdy beams of the bridge above. He couldn't help but compare the steel pillars to the bridges he had burned when he left the only life and family he had ever known. Had he been so naïve to think he could leave his old self behind without feeling the nagging guilt along the way?

Amidst the constant chatter of the bustling city, even at the late hour, he felt a deep ache toward the values that had been embedded in him since birth... family, community, and faith.

As his realization sank in, he knew he had to face up to who he really was, Amish roots and all. It was time to stop running, not just for his sake, but for Savannah's as well. The thought of her finding out this way, through a scandal and fallout, pained him more than personal ruin.

It dawned on him that no amount of distance or denial could change his roots or erase the core of who he was. If there were any hope of making things right, he would have to start with the truth—no matter how hard that might be. Only then could he work on restoring Savannah's trust and hopefully save his marriage. He only prayed she would still be there waiting for him when he was done facing his past.

Tracy Fredrychowski

CHAPTER 2

S avannah awoke with a start, her neck stiff and her eyes tight from an uneasy sleep on the sofa. The early morning light filtering in from the balcony window cast shadows on the kitchen stove clock that blinked six-thirty. Disoriented, she remembered waiting for Neal, each hour ticking by without his return. With a sinking feeling, she pushed herself off the couch and hurried to the bedroom, her heart pounding at what she might find.

The bedroom was just as she had left it the day before. The bed was neatly made, and Neals's pillow was untouched, a clear sign that he hadn't come home. Her stomach twisted with anxiety, and a wave of loneliness washed over her as she stood in the doorway.

Her phone lay on the coffee table, uncharged and as black as her heart felt. Rushing to plug it in, she noticed Neal's charger still dangling from the outlet on the counter.

With a heavy heart, she prepared for work, each motion devoid of the usual care she took in preparing for her day. Her hands trembled slightly as she poured herself a cup of coffee, her eyes constantly darting to her phone, which lay silent on the counter.

Savannah grabbed her keys and phone, tucking them into her purse. As she walked to her car, she replayed the unsettling events from the previous night in her mind. Holding a sliver of hope, she plugged the phone into the car's charger and breathed a sigh of relief when it came to life. Swiping through her messages, she saw one short message from Neal.

(Neal) *I'm fine, don't worry. I need to sort out a few things. I love you.*

Instead of replying, she tried calling him, but it went straight to voicemail. His message was cryptic and did little to soothe her spiraling thoughts. Why would he leave without giving her a proper explanation?

Determined to find some clues, she began calling some of his friends. He only had a few, and none of them had heard or seen him in days. His workplace was her last hope, but her call to his office deepened the mystery. He had taken some personal time, which he hadn't mentioned to her.

The situation went from worry to an edge of hostility that he would so carelessly disregard her feelings. Trying to maintain a façade of normalcy, Savannah went to work. Throughout the day, she stared blankly at her computer screen, her thoughts miles away or jumping down the throats of every team member who coursed through her doorway.

***

The following couple of weeks blurred into a series of sleepless nights and hazy days. Friends had called to express their concern; each call was a stab of a reminder of her current state of affairs. Her colleagues tiptoed around her, sensing her unpredictable mood.

Unable to bear the whispers for one more minute, she beckoned Jenna into her office and closed the door firmly behind them.

"Jenna, I need you to handle the one o'clock client meeting today," her voice was tense and to the point.

"Of course. Is everything alright? You seem… off lately."

Savannah tried to keep her emotions at bay, and the office was the last place she wanted to air her personal drama, but Jenna had always been a friend and confidant.

Filled with unease, she confessed, "It's Neal," her fingers twisting a pen at her desk. "He took off, and all I got from him was one simple text saying not to worry, that he had to take care of a few things. He won't answer my calls or reply to my messages. It's just not like him to disappear like this."

Jenna's expression shifted from professional concern to personal worry. "Oh, Savannah, that's… that's really strange. Did he say anything else, or where he might have gone?"

"That's it… nothing. I don't know what to do. It's like he just vanished."

Jenna sat in the chair across from her and leaned on her desk. "What about his family? Have you checked with them?"

Savannah shook her head. "That's a whole other story. I have no idea if he even has any living family or where they might be from. By his accent, they could live in Switzerland for all I know."

Jenna raised an eyebrow. "You've never met his family?"

"Nope… notta… no one."

Jenna sat back in her chair; her normal bubbly personality replaced with earnest seriousness. "He loves you, and I can't imagine him leaving for no good reason."

"I thought so too. But now I'm not sure about anything. He was my rock, and without him, everything feels off... out of balance."

Jenna patted the back of her hand supportively and added, "I'm sure there's a reasonable explanation for this. You wait and see."

Before Savannah could respond, her boss, Mr. Matthews, buzzed her into his office. Savannah's tone became serious as she rose from her desk, flipped her hair off her shoulder, and coldly said, "I best see what fire I need to put out before he pops a fuse."

As she made her way through the open-plan office, the rows of neatly lined desks seemed to blur, the murmurs of her colleagues fading to a distant hum. Just a few weeks ago, this was like her second home, but now, each cold and impersonal space added tension to her already burdened shoulders.

Entering Mr. Matthew's office, she was met with his frosty stare. The large, organized space felt colder than usual, and the walls lined with awards and photos of successful events were a harsh reminder of what he had demanded of his employees.

"Savannah, we lost the Campbell account," he stated bluntly, his sharp chin angled in a way that told her he wasn't happy. "They've decided to go with another agency. This was one of our largest clients, and their dissatisfaction seems to stem from a lack of communication and follow-up. What happened? You were in charge of that account."

Savannah's heart sank. She knew exactly what happened... *Neal*. She clasped her hands together, struggling to maintain professionalism against the rising tide of her panic and regret.

"I understand your concern, Mr. Matthews," she began, her voice hinting at the turmoil inside. "I'm sure I can smooth things over with them if given the chance." She squeezed her fingers together and looked him straight in the eye, hoping her honesty would help the dire situation. "I've been dealing with some personal issues, which momentarily impacted my work. I take full responsibility for the oversight."

Mr. Matthews leaned back in his chair, his expression cold and hard. "A personal emergency doesn't excuse losing a client as important as Campbell. I relied on your leadership, and this… it's unacceptable. Especially now with our expansion plans. I need a team leader I can count on, and you've proven you're not that person."

The sting of his words dug deep, igniting a firestorm of defensiveness within her. She felt her face flush with anger, and her heart pounded. Her voice, when she spoke, was laced with sarcasm. "With all due respect, my track record has always been 'up to par.' One oversight, while regrettable, hardly reflects my performance history." She paused, her breathing shallow, as she leaned forward, refusing to allow his demeanor to affect her argument. "I will rectify the situation."

"You'll do no such thing. Resolving this might be too late. Your disregard for duties has cost us dearly. This isn't about one client but the credibility of our entire operation. As of right now, it's best for the company if we part ways." He paused, his cold eyes lingering on her face as he held out his hand. "Your company keys."

She pulled a set of keys from her pocket as his words hit her like a dagger, leaving her momentarily breathless. Fired. Just like that. Her mouth went dry as she swallowed a fresh wave of anger. Without another word, she stood up, her chair scraping loudly against the floor in the silent office.

Her exit was swift and dramatic. As she strode through the array of desks, her heels clicked assertively against the floor, each step fueled by emotions. She held her head high, and her posture was rigid, not allowing the devastation to bend her, even as the reality of her sudden job loss began to sink in.

It only took a few minutes to gather a box of her personal things and head back through the center office. She felt her colleagues' eyes follow her, a mix of sympathy and awkward avoidance in their glances. She could feel their stares, unspoken questions, and whispered rumors already forming behind her back.

The full impact of what she'd lost began to sink in as she pressed the elevator call button. The elevator door dinged softly, its doors sliding open with a quiet whoosh. As she stepped inside, she leaned against the cool steel wall as it descended. Alone, she finally let the tears of shame run freely down her cheeks. Her sobs were silent but intense, each one a release of stress, hurt, and fear of what lay ahead.

***

The Greyhound bus groaned to a stop, its doors opening with a hiss that cut through the late-night air. Neal stepped off, his boots crunching the gravel of the small bus depot in Willow Springs, Pennsylvania. He breathed deeply; the smell of burning leaves and freshly spread manure covered him, transporting him back to a time of simplicity. It was the scent of home.

It had been three weeks since Neal made the agonizing decision to walk away from his life in Charleston, from Savannah, and from the lies that had sustained him there. The journey home had been a grueling test of wills. Choosing to travel with only the cash he had on him, Neal made brief stops along the way, picking up odd jobs to fund his travel to the next town. Each stop forced him to rediscover parts of himself that he had hidden away for too long.

In a small town in North Carolina, he found work on a cabbage farm. The sun beat down relentlessly as he picked cabbage alongside the farmer and his family. They were a lively bunch, their laughter and camaraderie filling the air as they worked. Neal was struck by the warmth and closeness of the family. They shared their meals with him, inviting him into their home as if he were one of their own.

One evening, as they gathered around the dinner table, the farmer's wife shared a story about their eldest son, who had recently moved away to college. Her eyes sparkled with pride, but there was a hint of sadness too. Neal felt a pang of longing. He missed the sense of belonging and the unconditional support of being part of a family.

"Family is everything," the farmer said, raising his glass in a toast. "No matter where you go or what you do, family should always be your anchor."

The words resonated deeply with Neal. At that moment, he realized how much he missed his family and the simple, unspoken bonds that held them together. As he left the farm, he carried with him a renewed sense of the importance of family.

During his second stop, he found himself in a small Amish community in Virginia, working for an elderly minister who needed help repairing his barn. The minister, an elderly man with a kind face and a gentle demeanor, often spoke of faith and trust in the Lord.

One afternoon, as they took a break, the minister asked, "You've been running from your past, haven't you?"

Neal nodded, feeling a lump in his throat. "I have. I've made so many mistakes."

The old man placed a hand on his shoulder. "We all make mistakes. It's not the mistakes that define us, but how we seek forgiveness in lieu of them. Trust in the Lord, and He will guide your steps."

The conversation lingered in Neal's mind as he continued his journey. He realized he had been relying on his own strength for too long, neglecting the faith that had once been a cornerstone of his life.

Before reaching Willow Springs, his final stop was in Pennsylvania, just a few towns south. There, he found work at a small community's general store. He helped stock shelves and made some minor repairs. The sense of community was evident; everyone knew each other and looked out for one another.

An elderly woman, Mrs. Yost, noticed Neal sitting alone on the small front porch and approached him.

"You're new here, aren't you?" she asked with a kind smile. "We always welcome new faces. I like to compare new people to a community, like a quilt. Every piece, no matter how small, is important."

Neal felt a deep sense of belonging as he listened to her words. He realized how much he missed being part of a community where everyone played a role and no one was left behind.

As Neal finally approached Willow Springs, his heart was heavy with the lessons he'd learned along the way. Family, faith, and community were the pillars he had neglected, and now was determined to rebuild his life around them. The journey had been long and tiring but had brought him much needed clarity. He was ready to face his past, seek forgiveness, and build a future grounded in the values he had rediscovered along the way.

Pulling his jacket tight to ward off the crisp night breeze, Neal looked up at the stars and wondered about Savannah. About how she was handling the sudden stress of his departure. With a heavy heart, he sent up a silent prayer for her safety and well-being, wishing he could offer more than prayers.

His cell phone, recently charged after long stretches of disuse, felt heavy in his hand as he scrolled through the numerous calls and messages from Savannah. He hesitated momentarily before typing out a message, his thumbs unsteady as he wrote: *"I'm safe. I think of you every day. I'm sorry for everything. I miss and love you. – Neal."* He hit send.

There was no undoing the past, but perhaps there could be understanding and forgiveness in time. For now, this was all he could offer, a simple assurance of his well-being and a token of his love. He then proceeded to power the phone off, hoping to preserve the battery as best he could.

Returning to his Amish community wasn't easy. He'd have to face why he left and find a way to rebuild the broken trust between his family and the church. But for the first time in weeks, as he walked down Main Street, he felt a spark of hope that perhaps this was where he needed to be to find the peace and simplicity he desperately sought.

***

Jobless and emotionally battered, Savannah found herself pacing the length of her living room, her movements swift as she dug through Neal's belongings, looking for any clue that might shed light on his mysterious past or where he might have gone.

Her frustration mounted with each item she picked up—a stack of magazines, a collection of business cards, and miscellaneous papers from work. He had always been so private about his life, skillfully changing the subject whenever she got too close to the truth. She hadn't thought much of it before, but now, looking back, he had created a well-constructed wall around his past that no one could climb, no matter how hard she tried.

Collapsing to the sofa with a stack of books in her lap, she sifted through each one, looking for anything to shed light on what he so craftily kept hidden. In his well-worn leather Bible, printed in a language she didn't understand, was a lone envelope addressed to Neal Zook. There was no return address, only a postmark of Pittsburgh to give a clue to its origin. Who was Neal Zook? The name struck her as odd since Zook wasn't a common name.

The postmark reminded her of the time when he had begged her to move to Pennsylvania, but she couldn't or wouldn't give up her job and home in Charleston. It was the only time he mentioned his parents and his need to be closer to them. That was a stressful time in their relationship. Neal had quit his job for no apparent reason, giving up everything he had worked so hard for. Nothing made sense then, and it certainly didn't make sense now. She was no closer to knowing where he might have gone, and her Internet searches gave her no clue about any of his family living anywhere near Pittsburgh.

As she sat there, she fingered through the thin pages, her eyes catching notes scribbled in the margins in Neal's handwriting. Passages underlined, words circled, a whisper of the man she thought she knew. One note, in particular, caught her attention. *"Seek truth, and you will find peace."* The neatly written comment stirred something inside her she didn't quite understand.

As she thought about their life together, she sensed that her husband had little peace. He always stood in the shadows of life, not fully committing himself to anyone or anything but her. But, even then, he pushed her away, not letting her share in whatever burden he was carrying.

There had been a time when he'd begged her to attend church with him. She'd always been too busy and didn't feel the need... but now, looking back, she couldn't help but wonder if her denial was why he felt he couldn't share whatever was bothering him.

Reading some of his most private thoughts in his Bible left her feeling empty and sad inside. Had she closed him off to his faith so much so that he couldn't allow her into his life?

Needing a breath of fresh air, she stepped onto the balcony, her isolation baring down on her shoulders. Neal was gone, her relationship with her parents strained, and her friends, busy with their own lives, had little time to console her broken heart. She felt all alone.

The warm evening air brushed against her skin as she slumped into a chair. The pretty city lights reflecting off the Ashley River didn't comfort her. She needed answers, not just for peace of mind, but also for her marriage and future.

Leaning her head back on the lounge chair, she let her eyes dance through the array of stars above. A tender moment suddenly surfaced—a cool summer evening, lying in the soft grass beside her Gigi. The sky was dotted with stars then, as it was now.

Gigi had always been her anchor, the one person who offered constant support through every twist and turn of her turbulent childhood. Her grandmother's sweet and gentle disposition was a startling contrast to her high-strung personality, yet her grandmother had a magical way of calming her down with just a few words. Every hug was like a burst of sunshine on the coldest days, leaving a lingering warmth that felt like a whispered promise that everything would be all right.

Even the thought of her grandmother brought a comforting embrace that eased the tension that had built up over the last few weeks, reminding her that she was the one person she could always count on for unconditional love. A sudden yearning to hear her voice forced her to pick up her phone. Just as she did, a text came in from Neal.

Her heart beat with hope as she saw Neal's name flash across the screen. Finally, she received a text from him. Her fingers trembled as she opened the message, and reading his brief words only angered her.

Without hesitation, she pressed the call button, her impatience growing as the call slipped straight to voice mail. Frustration welled inside her, drowning out the flicker of relief she had felt a moment ago.

"Why won't you pick up?" she screamed into the night. This cycle of short messages was torturous. She needed more than a couple of scraps of communication. She wanted answers, explanations, and something concrete to grasp.

In a rage, she threw her phone across the patio; it flew through the air before it bounced off the stucco wall with a sickening crack. She gasped, her anger turning to regret as she rushed to retrieve it.

The phone's screen was shattered, with spiderweb cracks across the surface, distorting the light from the still-lit display. Savannah picked it up gingerly, her heart sinking as she cradled the damaged device in her hands, pangs of remorse tightening her chest.

Taking a deep breath, she tried to compose herself. The phone lay in her lap, a reminder of her momentary loss of control and frustration. She needed to find another way to cope.

Again, the sweet face of her Gigi came to mind. It may be time to seek the comfort of her loving arms, if only for a few days.

Sitting there, she felt the warmth of the sticky salt air cover her, and a thought emerged, as clear as the promises her grandmother always whispered in her ear. *"You'll always have a place in my heart and home."*

Thoughts of her grandmother's quaint home deep in Amish country might just be what she needed. There, among the gentle buzz of rural living, she might find the clarity and peace she needed to maneuver the mess she called life.

Savannah picked up her phone and carried it back inside. The sudden coolness of the interior offered her little comfort against the turmoil boiling inside. Before heading to the bedroom, she remembered the stack of mail she had carried in that afternoon.

Sifting through the envelopes and flyers, her fingers paused on a thick envelope from the management of her condo complex. With a sinking feeling, she tore it open and unfolded its contents—a lease renewal notice, and a rent increase notification.

"Ugh!" she voiced loudly. Savannah let the papers slip from her fingers to the floor. Making her way to the bedroom, her movements were slow and heavy as she sat on the edge of her bed; the reality of losing yet another thing that meant so much to her came crashing down around her. Tears pooled in her eyes, and she looked around her beautifully decorated bedroom.

Collapsing back into the bed, she allowed herself to cry, once again mourning the loss of Neal, her job, and now her home. After the wave of emotions subsided, she lay in the quiet, staring at the ceiling. The practical side of her brain, ever the planner, began to piece together her limited options.

Extending her stay at Gigi's house wasn't just a temporary retreat anymore; it was a place where she could regroup. Perhaps at her grandmother's, surrounded by her comforting presence, she could find the strength to rebuild her life, one piece at a time.

CHAPTER 3

A few days later, Savannah stood near the patio door, light quivering at the horizon in an array of colors as the first rays of sun filtered over the Charleston landscape. She reached for her new phone, with the lease renewal was still scattered on the counter. Taking a deep breath, she dialed her grandmother's number.

The phone only rang once before Gigi's warm voice filled the line, soothing Savannah's frazzled soul. "Hello, my love," Gigi greeted, her tone conveying a smile.

"Hi, Gigi," her voice cracked under life's strain. "I... I was wondering if you'd like a visitor for a little while. I need some time away from the city... from everything here."

"Oh my, of course, I'd like nothing more. I've always told you you're always welcome in my home," Gigi replied without hesitation. "The country air and a change of scenery will do you good."

Savannah felt a wave of relief wash over her, and she was grateful for her grandmother's unconditional support. "Thank you. I need a chance to clear my head and find a way to get my life in order," she admitted, her voice trembling as she spoke.

"There, there, my dear," Gigi soothed. "It can't be all that bad."

"Oh, Gigi, you have no idea what I've been going through in the last few weeks."

Savannah told her grandmother everything that had transpired, and with each word, she felt her burden slightly lighten by being able to confide in someone who truly cared.

Her grandmother listened with a compassionate ear before sharing her perspective: "Remember, my dear, God often throws us storms to teach us strength. You come from a long line of strong women and are stronger than you think." Her grandmother gave her a moment to ponder her words before she continued. "God doesn't give us more than he has equipped us to handle, and he certainly doesn't leave us to weather the storms alone."

Savannah's thoughts briefly flickered to her mother, who had certainly weathered her share of storms. Though the thought of her mother stirred a difficult mix of emotions, she had to set them aside as her own life was spiraling out of control, demanding all the focus and energy she could muster to stay afloat.

With a churning of emotion, Savannah sighed softly into the phone, absorbing her grandmother's words. Deep down, she wished she could harness the kind of faith her grandmother lived by; a faith that seemed unshakable regardless of the challenges that came her way. "I wish I had your faith, Gigi."

Her grandmother slightly chuckled before responding, "Child, faith is like a muscle that grows stronger the more you use it," she explained. "You have it within you, my love. Use it, lean into it, and you'll see it won't fail you."

At a loss for words, Savannah could only believe that her grandmother was right and that, at some point, she'd know how to harness the level of faith she spoke of. The conversation then shifted to practical matters, with her grandmother's assurance she'd prepare the spare room for her arrival. As they said their goodbyes, Savannah had a renewed sense of purpose, a sliver of hope among the chaos.

Hanging up, Savannah looked around the condo, trying to determine what to take and what to store away. She clung to her grandmother's words as she sorted through her belongings. Perhaps in Pennsylvania, in the embrace of her grandmother's warmth, she could find the strength to see the assurance of God in her life... something she'd all but ignored since entering adulthood.

***

Just as the clock struck midnight, Neal finally arrived at his parent's home. The old farmhouse, nestled under century-old maple trees, seemed frozen in time. A wooden swing, still secured to the largest limb of the tree just outside his bedroom window, dangled in time as he looked around the moonlit yard. Memories came flooding back, leaving him with a sense of remorse and an overwhelming sadness at what he'd given up when he chose to run away from all he knew.

Despite the hour, he yearned to knock on the door, see his parents' faces, and end the years of silence; instead, he headed to the barn to find rest in the hayloft.

Making his way to the barn, he was reminded of the time when he almost came home one other time. He'd quit a job when intense background checks were instated. He was then determined to face his past, but without Savannah's support in moving, he hid another layer of his past and stayed put in the life he created.

The heavy barn door creaked softly as he opened it, the familiar scent of hay and livestock welcoming him home. Climbing the stairs and settling into the soft hay, he heaved a weary sigh. The occasional neigh of the buggy horses below filled the air, reminding him of the severity of what his return would mean to his family.

Folding his hands under his head, he stared at the rough beams of the barn roof. There, in the quiet of the night, he relived the events that forced him from his life, and the barriers he had built to protect himself started to crumble. He was finally home, even if it meant he might lose Savannah in the process.

The teenage prank—that fretful night—flashed vividly in his mind. What had started as a foolish stint of rebellion had ended in tragedy: the loss of three of his friends in a horrific accident that had shaken his family and the entire Amish community. He'd never been able to forgive himself for his role and the decision to keep the truth hidden. The weight of his guilt had driven him away from his Amish roots, and away from those who might have helped him heal.

The unbearable silence at the breakfast table the morning after the news broke out, the looks of sorrow, and the whispers of the community followed him everywhere he went. It was just too much for him to bear. Fleeing seemed the only way to escape the judgment and self-loathing. He ran far and fast away from everything that reminded him of home. He didn't want remnants of his prior life to spill over into the new life he had built in Charleston.

Now, as the soft sounds of the farm settled around him, he realized the enormity of the task ahead. He needed to confront his past and seek forgiveness not just from his family but also from himself. It was a chance to set things right; to rebuild the bridges he'd burned in his haste to escape the pain.

As the night deepened, his eyes finally closed, with visions of Savannah ever so prevalent behind his darkened lids. The rhythmic breathing of the animals finally lulled him into a restful sleep.

***

After a couple of days of packing, Savannah stood in the middle of her nearly empty condo, surrounded by the last of the moving boxes she was taking to Pennsylvania with her. The rest of her belongings had already been sold or transported to a rented storage unit nearby. The spacious condo now echoed with a hollow sound of emptiness, each noise amplifying her unknown future.

She made a final walk-through, trying to hold on to the last lingering memories of her life with Neal. It was hard to leave and accept that she was doing it alone. But the conversation with her grandmother had planted a new seed of hope and determination within her.

With a deep, steady breath, she picked up the phone and called her grandmother. "Hi, Gigi, it's all set. I'll be leaving in a few minutes and should be there sometime late this evening."

"I can't wait to see you." Gigi's voice trickled with warmth and sincerity. "Drive safe, and remember, there's no rush. You stop if you get tired. I'm not going anywhere. I'll be here when you arrive."

Savannah's heart swelled with gratitude. "Thank you, Gigi. I... I really need this," she admitted, trying to hide the quaver in her voice.

"A visit with family will do wonders to soothe the soul. And remember, you're not running from your problems. You're heading to a place where you can find healing."

Encouraged by her grandmother's words, Savannah felt another flicker of optimism in her sea of overwhelming worry.

As she placed the last few items in a box, she lingered on Neal's well-worn German Bible. While she didn't understand his underlined words, she read some handwritten notes along the margins. Despite their distance and silence, each word seemed to connect her with her husband.

Balancing the last box on her hip, she shut the door to start her journey back to Pennsylvania. She couldn't help but hope that in the quiet of her grandmother's home, she could find the clarity to face whatever the future held.

***

As dawn broke, Neal roused to the sound of a rooster calling in a new day. His body was stiff from the night spent on the loft floor, but his determination was firm. It was time to face his parents and the years of pain that lay between them.

Walking toward the house, his heart pounded with dread and anticipation. He prayed they'd welcome him home. The familiar creak of the porch steps seemed louder in the morning stillness. As he raised his hand to knock, the smell of strong coffee and bacon made his stomach remember the comfort of his mother's cooking.

He hesitated momentarily before the door swung open. His father stood there, the lines on his face deeper than he remembered, but his eyes filled with recognition and apprehension filtered across his brow.

"Neal…" his father mumbled.

"*Datt*," he managed, his own voice choked with emotion.

At that moment, his mother appeared behind his father. Her gasp was audible, a hand flying to cover her mouth as tears sprang to her eyes. She wasted no time pushing past his father to engulf Neal in her arms. "You're home, you're finally home," her voice was muffled against his chest.

Neal hugged her tightly, allowing her clean scent to fill his mind with a wave of fresh memories. "I'm sorry for everything."

"We thought we might never see you again," his mother cried, holding him back at arm's length to look at him. "We've prayed every day for your safe return."

They stood on the porch for a long moment, a family reunited in the wake of past sorrows, his mother's warm embrace healing the silent wounds of his absence. Eventually, they stepped inside the kitchen's warmth, shaking off the cool fall morning air.

As they gathered around the old wooden table, the comforting smell of breakfast filled the air as his mother bustled about. His father sat silently across from him; his face unreadable under the tension simmering just below the surface.

Finally, his father broke the silence. "It's good to see you," he began, his voice tense, "but I can't help but wonder what your intentions are now that you've returned."

Neal felt the sting of his father's words. He knew this confrontation was inevitable, yet harder than he anticipated. "I'm here because I want to make things right."

His father's eyes narrowed, skepticism etched across his weathered face. "It'll take more than a short visit to restore harmony to this family and our community."

Neal's mother, sensing the rising tension, paused her work, her expression anxious as she looked between them. Yet she remained silent, knowing the importance of the conversation.

Neal swallowed hard, the fear of rejection from his father clawing at his chest. "I can't change the past. All I can do is show you I want to make amends... whatever that looks like." He paused and waited to see if his father would add anything before continuing, "I'm not asking for your immediate trust. I know I'll need to earn that back over time."

With a measure of reluctance, his father leaned back in his chair and ran a hand through his long, graying beard. "You're right about that. Trust is earned, and it'll take time. But you're still my son, and that counts for something." He picked up his coffee and swallowed a mouthful before adding, "There's a lot of unanswered questions milling about."

His mother set a plate of food in front of Neal and tenderly patted his shoulder before returning to the stove. Her silent gesture warmed Neal's heart as he waited for her to take her seat. "*Jah*, I know, and I've come to share the answers."

As they continued to talk, the undercurrent of tension remained, a reminder of the delicacy of their relationship and the effort required to mend it. If it weren't for his mother's comforting presence, he might have chosen to leave without any hope of reconciliation.

Sensing the need to lighten the mood and bring a sense of normalcy back to the conversation, Neal proceeded cautiously. "There's also something else I should tell you both. I got married while I was away."

His mother perked up, eager to grasp positive news, but his father remained stoic. "Tell us about her," his mother pleaded. "What community is she from?"

Neal sucked in a silent breath, trying to keep his tone neutral, aware of his father's reaction as he gathered enough nerve to break the news that Savannah was *Englisch*. "I met her in Charleston. That's where I've been living for the last five years. She's not Amish, though, which I know might be hard to understand. But she means a lot to me."

"Ohhh…" her mother whispered, disappointment evident in her tone.

The silence following his mother's whispered reaction stretched, filling the room with unsaid thoughts and concerns.

"She's… she's different from what you might be used to here," Neal continued, choosing his words carefully. "Savannah has a determined spirit, a quality that has made her incredibly successful in her career. She's not shy about expressing her opinions, and she has a confidence that's... well, it's quite something to see."

His father raised an eyebrow. "That's not typically how women handle themselves around here."

Neal nodded, acknowledging the truth in his father's words. "I know, and it did take me some time to adjust. But her strength is one of the things I admire most about her. She is also incredibly smart and caring. She has a big heart and shows it in the most unexpected ways."

His mother was still processing the news, whose eyes seemed to soften slightly. "And she accepts your Amish roots?" her voice etched with concern.

Neal hesitated, the burden of his lies pressing down on him. "She... she doesn't know," he admitted, looking down at his hands, feeling the shame creep up his neck.

His parents exchanged a look that carried disappointment and understanding that only those who deeply knew each other could share.

Neal's confession hung heavy in the air as his parents remained silent. His mother's expression was pained. She paused to tidy up the kitchen, and it was a few moments before she spoke again.

"You mean to say she doesn't even know you're Amish?" she asked; her tone littered with disbelief. "How could you keep something so important hidden from her? That's not just a small detail: it's who you are."

Before thinking twice about his words, Neal boldly added, "It's who I was. Not who I am now."

His father's expression hardened. He leaned forward, his eyes locking on Neal's, searching for an explanation in his son's troubled gaze. "That's a serious omission. You've not only left your community, but you also left your truth behind," his father said sternly. "Trust is the foundation of a relationship. What do you plan to do about this?"

Neal knew he deserved every bit of the reprimand. "I know I've made yet another huge mistake," he muttered low. "I was scared that she might see me differently if she knew about my background. But I realize now that I've only made things worse by not being honest with her from the start."

His mother sat back down, folded her hands, and leaned in. "Son, love isn't just about accepting the easy parts of someone; it's about embracing all of it, even the parts that are hard to understand. You need to give her the chance to accept you for who you are—Amish roots and all."

Neal appreciated his parents' support despite his failings. In time, he clung to the hope that Savannah would eventually find it in her heart to give him a second chance. Yet he knew he needed to make amends with his community before asking for forgiveness and regaining her respect.

***

Neal sat on the worn wooden steps of his parent's front porch as he watched the neighbor across the road lead his Belgium work horses around the field, cutting the last of the hay before the cold set in. The smell of fresh-cut grass took him back to a time when he and his *bruder* followed their *datt* around the field as they picked up bundles and set shocks of wheat to dry.

Binding wheat was a hot and tiring job, but at the end of the day, *Mamm* would offer them glasses of meadow tea, and they would sit and plan how long it would take the wheat to dry before taking it to the threshing machine. A steady hard work his body ached for, and a time lost forever... or as it seemed.

His thoughts were interrupted by the steady thud of boots approaching. He didn't need to look up to know it was his younger *bruder*, David. Younger by just one year, David had a noticeable limp from a farm accident that occurred ten years earlier.

David stopped a few feet away, his form stiff against the backdrop of their mother's tidy flower garden. His eyes were unyielding as they landed on Neal, who had looked up to meet his glare.

"So, you decided to show your face around here again," David said, his voice tight with sarcasm.

"Good to see you too." Neal groaned. "I'm here to—"

"Save it, Neal," David cut him off sharply. "You left us. After everything that happened… after Joe, Eli, and Samuel… you just ran away without explanation. And now what? You stroll back here like nothing happened, expecting what? Forgiveness?"

Neal stood up to face David, who was noticeably a few inches taller now. "I'm not expecting immediate forgiveness. I know what I did was wrong. I'm here to make amends… to give closure to those who need it."

David snorted, shaking his head as he looked out over the farm. "You think you can just come back and make everything right? It's been years of dealing with the whisperers, dealing with our friend's families needing answers, and you were nowhere to be found to give them what they needed."

"I understand that," Neal replied as he kicked a stone with the toe of his boot. "I've lived with the guilt every day, and it's torn me up inside. That's why I'm back to seek forgiveness from my family and the community... from everyone I've hurt."

With unsure eyes, David shook his head. "And how do you plan to do that? Just walk up and say... look I'm sorry your boy died on account of me?"

Neal nodded solemnly. "If that's what it takes. I'll go to each family, explain what really happened that night, and accept whatever they decide. I owe them that much." His voice was steady, but his stomach churned with the thought of the task ahead.

"You've got a long road to walk. And I can't speak for anyone else, but..." David paused. "I wouldn't want to be in your shoes. The night those boys died left a scar on this community, not so easily forgotten."

A lump formed in Neals's throat at David's warning, and he had to swallow hard before replying. "I'm ready to face them, to finally speak the truth. I can't change the past, I know that, but I can't move on until I at least ask for forgiveness for the part I played in their deaths."

"You know as well as I do," David began, "that we believe that every life and death is by *Gott's* will, in His exact timing. While you've been away, most families have found peace in that. They've mourned but also accepted it was in *Gott's* plan… they've moved on. I'm afraid what dredging up all those old memories will do now."

Neal listened; the familiar doctrine mingled with his own emotions. "I respect their faith and their process of healing. But I also know that my running away left unanswered questions, and maybe I'm the one who can't move on until they hear what I have to say."

David's eyes lingered on Neal's for a moment before he added, "I just hope that while you've come to terms with your own guilt, it won't reopen old wounds. Be prepared for that. Not everyone may be ready to hear what you have to say, no matter your intentions." With that, David turned and walked away, leaving Neal alone to face his unsettled thoughts.

CHAPTER 4

The miles stretched endlessly before Savannah as she drove up Interstate 77, the scenery shifting from Charleston's low country marshes to the rolling hills of the Appalachian foothills. Her car hummed along the highway, but her mind was anything but calm. The eleven-hour journey to Willow Springs provided her plenty of time to reflect—too much time, she thought bitterly.

Glancing at the empty passenger seat, memories of Neal flooded her mind: his laughter, the way he teased her about her high-strung nature, the gentle kisses that spoke of promises and forever. But now, those memories did nothing but intensify her pain, especially with his empty seat staring back at her. She often wondered why he had no desire to learn to drive, but again, she liked to be in control, so she didn't mind.

"Why didn't I insist he tell me more about his past?" she muttered, gripping the steering wheel tighter. The question tugged at her heart, each mile increasing her frustration. "I was so caught up in him that I just accepted his vague answers, didn't I?" she asked herself. "Like a fool... now I'm paying the price for my naivety."

She felt anger building inside her, a slow-burning fire smoldering since the day he left. The more she thought about it, the more it consumed her every thought. Her frustration reached a boiling point when she pulled off at a rest area. The car's engine ticked as it cooled, and she sat there for a moment, her heart pounding with pent-up rage and hurt.

Grabbing her phone, she opened her text messages and typed furiously. *"How could you do this to me? I deserve to know where you are and why you left. How can you write me off like our marriage meant nothing? I thought you loved me. This isn't love; this is heartless. If pushing me away is your idea of marriage, I want nothing to do with it or you ever again!"*

Her finger hovered over the send button for a second, her mind racing with conflicting emotions. But the anger won out, and she hit send, watching the message fly off into the void. For a fleeting moment, she felt a sense of justification wash over her.

But the satisfaction was short-lived. As the minutes ticked by, regret set it. What if her harsh words pushed him further away? What if she made things worse? She stared at her phone, willing it to show a response, a sign indicating he was out there, that he cared enough to reply.

When she rechecked his location, she was met with the same frustrating result... his phone's location services were still turned off. There was no clue, no hint of his whereabouts. It was as if he had vanished completely from her life.

"Why Neal? Why won't you talk to me?" she whispered, tears pooling on her bottom lashes. The anger flared again, mixing with twinges of regret, leaving her feeling helpless and alone all over again.

She leaned back in her seat, staring at the steady stream of cars pulling into the parking lot, reminding her of the journey she must continue. But the road ahead felt daunting.

With a sense that she would crack at any moment, she started the car and pulled back onto the highway, her mind swirling with thoughts and emotions she didn't want to deal with. As the miles ticked away, she was determined to face whatever lay ahead with the same fiery spirit that had carried her thus far.

***

The sun had started its descent behind the horizon as Savannah pulled off Interstate 79 at the Grove City exit. The familiar landscape stirred memories of visiting Willow Springs, especially spending time with her Amish friend Sarah Byler.

The thought of Sarah's unwavering friendship brought a sudden ache to her heart. She yearned for her friend, who was grounded in honesty and warmth, far removed from the superficial ties she had left behind in Charleston.

A warm smile came to Savannah's face as she recalled Sarah's way of speaking with compassion and truth, unafraid to tackle the deeper issues of life and faith. Not that she herself ever had much say about faith issues, but she loved how Sarah spoke clearly about her trust in the Lord.

While her Charleston friends were lively and entertaining, they seemed more concerned with social standing and gossip than genuine matters of the heart. The mere difference between these friendships made her realize how much she longed for the kind of soul-nurturing relationship she once had with Sarah.

As she navigated the gentle curves of Route 208, the rolling hills and neatly kept farms of Willow Springs brought a surprising sense of peace. Slowing down behind a brown-capped buggy, she felt a moment of stillness that eased the tension built up over her long drive. The rhythmic clip-clop of the horse's hooves and the gentle sway of the buggy brought a smile to her face. As she carefully drove around the slow-moving buggy, she caught the eye of a little girl peeking out from the back. The child's innocent smile and cheerful wave melted away the last remnants of her anger and frustration, replacing them with tender warmth.

As Savannah pulled into her grandmother's driveway, the sight that greeted her was not what she remembered from a few years earlier. The old home, nestled among sprawling maple trees, seemed to have surrendered to its age. The paint faded more than she recalled, and the porch sagged slightly, needing repair. A feeling of apprehension tightened her chest as she exited her car.

Something tugged at her heart as she took in the simplicity of her grandmother's home—very different from her well-appointed condo back in Charleston. The reality of what she was stepping into sank in. She took a long breath and braced herself for the culture shock she was about to bear.

Could she really exchange her posh, modern lifestyle for life here, in a house that, if memory served correctly, smelled of the essential oils her grandmother insisted on using?

Walking up the creaky steps to the front door, Savannah felt a sense of nostalgia and misgivings. The door opened before she could knock, revealing Gigi's smiling face, which glowed with warmth and welcome. "Savannah, my love!" her grandmother exclaimed, her arms opened wide.

As they embraced, Savannah breathed in the familiar scent of lavender and linen, which somehow overpowered the smell of the old house seeping out the open door. Gigi's hug brought a surge of comfort, reminding her of the summers spent in this place, filled with love and carefree days with her grandparents.

"It's good to see you, Gigi," Savannah said as she stepped into her embrace.

"Oh, let me take a look at you!" Gigi stepped back, her eyes sparkling as she took in her city-polished appearance. "You look so grown up. But you look tired, dear. Come in, come in."

As they entered the living room, Savannah couldn't help but notice the simple furnishings and fading curtains, each corner a memory from the past pulled from somewhere lost in time.

Gigi must have noticed her pause. "I know it's not much," she began, pointing to the chairs positioned perfectly around the small table in the center of the kitchen, "it's a bit more rustic than your fancy lifestyle."

Savannah smiled, accepting her invitation. "It's not that. It's just a lot to take in. The house seems... different from what I remember."

Gigi nodded, understanding. "Time hasn't been kind to the old place, especially now that your grandfather's gone. But I manage, but it's a lot for one old lady to keep up with."

Savannah tried to relax, the warmth of the kitchen comforting her. "Maybe I can help with a few things. It might help me get my mind off my troubles."

Gigi chuckled softly. "That's my girl. Fixing up this old house might heal us both. We've got plenty of time and tea for the problems we need to sort through." She reached across the table and squeezed her hand. "I've missed you. It's been too quiet... too empty around here... especially since your grandfather left us."

When her grandmother got up to turn on the teapot, Savannah couldn't help but feel a twinge of disappointment. "I'm surprised Dad hasn't been here more to help out. He only lives an hour away."

Gigi's face softened with a sad smile. "Your father has his own life, my dear. The divorce was hard on him, and the last thing he needs is to worry about this old place. Your father has his own burdens to cross, and I've made peace with that long ago."

A pang of guilt for her own lack of interest settled between her grandmother's words. "Still, that's no excuse." However, inside, Savannah knew the struggles her father endured, and she was sure he didn't know the extent of his mother's home condition. If he did, she was sure he would've addressed the issues before now.

"Now, child, get that worried look off your face. People take care of me. I live in a wonderful, caring community that looks after widows like myself. I want for nothing or need of nothing except the companionship of my granddaughter and an occasional visit from my son."

Savannah shook her head, determination setting in. "Well, that's beside the point. This house and you deserve better. We'll get this place back in shape in no time."

Gigi's eyes sparkled with gratitude. "You don't have to do that, dear. But I appreciate your willingness to help. This house could use some tender loving care."

Savannah glanced around the kitchen, imagining the possibilities. "We'll start with the porch. Perhaps we can find someone to fix the sagging railing and add a fresh coat of paint to the exterior." Savannah looked around the kitchen. "We'll tackle the interior, one room at a time. It will be a lot of work, but I think it will be good for the both of us."

Her grandmother wiped the moisture from the corner of her eyes with a lacy hankie tucked up under the sleeve of her sweater. "You've always had a strong spirit, just like your mother. She was always determined to make things better as well."

Savannah's expression tightened at the mention of her mother. "It feels like she drifted away from all of us after she and Dad split up." Savannah paused to push away the harsh reality of her parent's past, silently hoping she and Neal weren't headed in the same direction.

"Your mother has her own journey to walk," Gigi said gently. "I learned long ago that I can only be responsible for my own path. And right now, it seems our paths have brought us together, and that's all we must be concerned about today."

Savannah smiled at her grandmother's way of turning a touchy subject, like her parents, into a warm embrace of acceptance.

Settling into bed later that evening, childhood memories pressed heavily against her chest. The lingering impact of her parents' divorce had left deep emotional scars, reminding her that she, too, might one day need to reconcile with the very people who had shaped her early years.

Snuggling under the heavy quilt to ward off the chill of the drafty house, Savannah marveled at her grandmother's remarkable ability to accept and forgive her parents' shortcomings with such grace. The warmth of Gigi's unconditional love and understanding was a light amid her own wavering emotions. One day, she hoped to extend the same heartfelt forgiveness to her parents, embracing their flaws and mistakes with the same compassion that Gigi had shown.

***

Neal was helping David stack hay bales in the barn when he felt his phone buzz in his pocket. With a quick glance to ensure David wasn't watching, he pulled out the phone and read the message from Savannah. Her words cut through like a knife:

"How could you do this to me…"

His heart ached as he read her bitter words. He knew his wife, and she often reacted before she thought. He was sure she was venting, but the pain in the message was undeniable, making the barn feel suddenly stifling.

David must have noticed the change in his stance, and quickly asked, "Something wrong?"

Neal pocketed the phone, trying to mask his distress. "It's nothing, just… just a lot on my mind."

David frowned. "A lot on your mind, huh? You've been back for less than a few days, and you still seem like a walking time bomb about ready to explode."

Neal hesitated; Savannah's text still fresh in his mind. Finally, he decided to open up, the words spilling out in a rush. "I changed my identity. Took on a new name, a new life. And it cost me everything. I lost my job because of it, and I couldn't face what I'd done. That's why I ran, and I couldn't bear to tell her the truth about who I was and what I'd done."

David's eyes widened in shock. "You changed your identity? Why on earth would you do that? Are you ashamed of who you were?"

For a moment, shame was evident in his voice. "I wanted to escape everything that reminded me of what happened here, of the accident, about what I'd done. I thought if I could be someone else and start fresh, I wouldn't have to deal with the guilt and pain."

"*Ach,*" David grunted as he heaved another hay bale toward him.

Neal nodded as beads of sweat burned his eyes. "I know. I'm not proud of it. And it gets worse. I falsified my onboarding documents that were sent to a government contract company, and I could be in serious trouble."

David's expression soured. "And you brought this trouble back here. How could you? You're not just dealing with family issues; you've got legal problems that could catch up with you too?"

"That's one of the reasons why I left Charleston and came home. I hoped to find some peace here, to sort things out away from the mess I created."

Neither brother spoke a word for the next few minutes until Neal admitted. "I'm married. The text was from my wife." Making a guttural sound, more truth spilled out. "I didn't want to bring her into all of this until I had a chance to face my past and sort all this out. She doesn't know where I am, and she doesn't know about my Amish background."

David removed his straw hat and wiped his forehead with the back of his hand before saying, "You can't keep running."

David barely let him catch his breath before throwing another hay bale at him. He felt the mass of David's words on his shoulders as he said. "I know I need to make things right, but I don't even know where to start."

David hollered slightly sarcastically, "How about with the truth?"

As they continued to work, the fear of his past catching up with him lingered in the stagnant, dusty barn air. Each time a car passed by his father's driveway, his heart skipped a beat, anxiety tightening its grip as his mind raced with possibilities… could this be the moment everything caught up with him?

***

The next morning, Savannah's comfort level was put to the test. She was jolted awake by the sound of a baby crying. Groggy and disoriented, she quickly emerged from her bedroom, the old wooden floorboards creaking under her feet.

She found Gigi in the living room, cradling an infant, who was wailing loudly. "Oh, Savannah, you're up," Gigi exclaimed over the baby's cries. "This is Harry. He's Reuben and Allie Raber's child. I watch him when Allie needs to help out in the apple barn."

Savannah rubbed her eyes, trying to shake off the remnants of sleep. "I didn't know you babysat," she said, voice still thick with sleep.

Gigi smiled warmly, gently rocking the fussy baby in her arms. "Would you like to hold him?"

Savannah held up a hand to push the idea away. "Heaven's no! I need coffee and a shower before I do anything."

Gigi led Savannah into the kitchen, where the sun streamed through the thin curtains. "Let me show where the coffee is and where fresh towels are." As they moved through the house, her grandmother pointed to a throw on the end of the bed. "This blanket was crocheted by your great-grandmother." Gigi gently ran her fingers over the intricate stitches as if she recalled a sweet memory. "And this dresser belonged to your grandfather. He built it himself."

Savannah tried to hide her discomfort as she noticed the true condition of the outdated bathroom with its clawfoot tub and lack of modern fixtures. She didn't know why such things hadn't bothered her as a child, but at that moment, she felt like she was falling through a dark hole with no place to land.

After a bath, the small, cramped kitchen that looked bigger last night, with its ancient stove and limited counter space, was a far cry from the sleek and modern kitchen she left behind. Suddenly realizing her grandmother's house didn't have an automatic coffee maker, she listened patiently as her grandmother explained how to use the percolator on top of the stove. Her attempt to use the old stove was met with minor frustration as she struggled to figure out the knobs and how to light the fire beneath the porcelain pot. In addition—the lack of outlets and no Internet added to her sense of displacement.

"Gigi, how do you manage with so few outlets?" she asked, trying to keep her tone respectable despite her growing frustration.

Her grandmother giggled. "What do I need outlets for? I don't have a television, only a few lights when I need them, and everything else I need is either wind-up or battery-operated. You'll get used to it." Her grandmother paused and smiled, with a knowing grin. "Eventually, you'll find the joy in the simplicity."

Savannah turned to pour herself a cup of coffee, rolled her eyes, and mumbled, "I highly doubt that."

"What was that? Did you say something?" her grandmother asked.

"Oh… no, Gigi, just trying to find my way around."

After laying baby Harry down, Gigi met her at the window as she stared out over her garden with its neat and tidy rows. A few red tomatoes clung to their withering vines, and brown corn stocks were stacked in a tight bundle against the fence.

"I spend a lot of my time there," Gigi said, her eyes twinkling with pride. "It's my little sanctuary."

"I used to love helping you in the garden, remember?" Savannah asked.

"I do. We planted a whole row of sunflowers just for you one year. I still plant them today, remembering the summers you spent with us."

Her grandmother pointed to the far side of the garden. "See, over there. Their flowerheads are just about dry. Soon, I'll bring them in and shuck the seeds to feed the birds this winter."

They turned from the window and sat at the table, and Gigi added, "Maybe we can plant two rows next year. One for you and one for me."

The suggestion hung in the air, and suddenly, Savannah was hit with a cold wave by the thought of living with her grandmother through the winter. The idea of staying that long was overwhelming. A sense of panic began to bubble up inside her, and she found it hard to keep her composure.

Just as she felt her face cracking, little Harry let out a piercing cry, breaking the tension in the room. Savannah breathed a silent sigh of relief, grateful for the distraction. Her grandmother's hopeful expression was hard to face, and she was thankful for any excuse to avoid showing the panic that swarmed over her.

"Oh, Harry, what's the matter?" Gigi cooed, moving to pick up the wailing infant.

Savannah took a deep breath, trying to steady her racing thoughts. "I'll hold him now, Gigi," she said as she reached for the baby. Anything to keep her hands busy and her mind off the daunting prospect of an extended stay in Willow Springs.

His cries softened as she cradled the baby, but Savannah's mind was still in turmoil. The small kitchen, outdated appliances, and mere bleakness of everything around her... felt so foreign. The thought of enduring an entire winter was almost too much to bear.

"Gigi," Savannah began, her voice trembling, "I'm not sure how I'll manage all this. It's just so different from what I'm used to."

Her grandmother reached across the table and patted the back of her arm. "I know it's a big change. But sometimes, change is exactly what we need to find new strength and purpose. You don't need to do it all at once. Take one day at a time."

With the now quiet baby in her arms, she snuggled into his fresh baby scent, feeling a tiny spark of the courage her grandmother believed she had.

CHAPTER 5

The early morning light filtered through the orange and red maple leaves that hung over Gigi's front porch. Savannah sat in a weathered rocking chair; a blanket wrapped around her shoulders to ward off the cool fall air. With a steaming cup of coffee, she breathed in its fresh aroma as she marveled at the quiet start of a new day.

As she watched the day unfold, Savannah's thoughts drifted to the previous evening, when she had unpacked the last of her boxes and explored the nooks and crannies of her bedroom. She had stumbled upon an old shoebox filled with letters and photographs, revealing a part of her grandmother's past she knew nothing about.

After placing her cup aside, she began sifting through the shoebox she carried to the porch. Each letter told a story of her grandmother's struggles, vividly depicting her past and the forbidden love she shared with her grandfather.

Gigi soon joined her, carrying a plate of warm cinnamon rolls. "Good morning, my dear," she said, setting their breakfast between them. "You're up early. Did you sleep well?"

Savannah smiled as she accepted the sweet-smelling treat. "I slept okay but couldn't stop thinking about these," she gestured toward the shoebox on her lap. "I found them in the bottom drawer of my dresser. I never knew you had an Amish past."

Gigi's eyes softened as she looked at the box. "Ah, those old letters. They hold many memories, some sweet and some bittersweet. I suppose it's time you knew more about your roots."

Savannah's curiosity deepened. "Why didn't Dad ever mention any of this to me? It feels like a whole part of our history was hidden away."

Gigi struggled to keep her voice steady and settled into the rocking chair beside her. "Your father had his reasons. After he left for the military, he found it difficult to stay connected to his roots. It was easier to distance himself than face the reason why he couldn't stay in Willow Springs."

"What reasons could be so bad he couldn't share this part of our history with me?" Savannah inquired.

"Maybe someday he'll share it with you... matters of the heart are his story to tell, not mine."

Savannah looked down at the letters, emotions swirling within her. "I understand why he might have felt that way, but it feels like I've been kept in the dark about so many things."

Gigi reached over and placed a comforting hand on her arm. "Relationships are never easy, especially with family. Understanding where we come from sometimes helps us find our way forward."

As Savannah sifted through the old box, her eyes caught a faded newspaper article about a group of Amish men building a barn. Her heart skipped a beat when she noticed a familiar face among them. The bare-faced young man stood out against the bearded men in the photo, his resemblance to Neal uncanny.

"Gigi, who's this?" Savannah asked, holding the discolored paper out. "This man... he looks so familiar."

Gigi peered at the article, studying it intently. "If my memory serves me right, that's Harold and Priscilla Zook's oldest boy, Neal." Her grandmother paused before explaining the article. "A neighbor's barn burned down, and it was all over the papers; people were amazed at how the community came together to rebuild the barn so quickly."

Gigi glanced over at Savannah and quickly stood. "Oh my! Could it be?" The older woman scrambled back into the house and was back on the porch just as quickly, carrying Savannah's wedding picture. "I always said Neal reminded me of someone, but I couldn't remember. It's him. Neal Zook is your husband, isn't he?"

The box slid off Savannah's lap, scattering the letters across the porch as she pulled the faded newspaper clipping closer, her eyes wide. "Gigi, that's my Neal in the photo. He has a beard now, but I'm certain it's him."

Gigi leaned in, looking closer at the photo. "It is, I'm certain. There's no mistaking those eyes."

Savannah nodded, her heart pounding. "Yes, I'm sure. This explains a few things... especially his accent; I could never quite place it, but now it makes sense. I want to know why he never told me about this part of his life."

Savannah took a deep breath, her mind racing and a new surge of anger rising to her chest. "I need to talk to him. Where do the Zooks live? Maybe they know where he is."

Gigi must have sensed her building agitation because she put a loving hand on her knee, holding her back from getting up.

"Savannah, my dear, I know you're upset, but you must approach this delicately. The Zooks are Old Order Amish, and they won't take kindly to a fiery young English girl showing up on their porch demanding answers about their long-lost son."

Savannah's eyes darted to her car and back to the newspaper photo. "Long lost my foot. I know exactly where he's been. He ran off and married me! And I have every right to know where he is."

Gigi squeezed her knee, her voice soothing. "I understand, my dear, but you must be careful. Neal's past and his family's way of life are deeply rooted in tradition and faith, and they don't take kindly to outsiders."

"I'm no outsider, Gigi, I'm his wife,"

Gigi nodded sympathetically. "If he's truly Harold Zook's boy, he must have had his reasons for not sharing this part of his life with you."

Savannah took a long breath through her nose and closed her eyes, leaning on the back of the chair. "I just don't understand why he couldn't trust me with the truth. We're supposed to be partners, and he kept this huge part of his life hidden from me."

"Sometimes people keep secrets not to deceive but to protect the ones they love."

Savannah's shoulders sagged slightly. "Is that what you and Dad did by keeping your Amish roots from me?"

Her grandmother had no words, only giving her a gentle nod in response.

Savannah's emotions triggered an array of unbecoming reactions to her grandmother's gentle manner. She stood abruptly, the old wooden chair scraping against the porch floor. "Why does everyone think I can't handle the truth?"

Gigi looked up, concern etched on her aging features. "I know you need answers, but storming off won't help. You must give your mind time and prayer to process it all."

Savannah's eyes flashed with defiance. "I need answers, Gigi. I'll leave the praying to you. I can't just sit here and wait. I'm going to the market, and then I'm heading to the Zook farm."

Gigi stood, reaching out a hand of warning. "Please, Savannah, show them the respect they deserve even if you're upset."

Savannah laid a reassuring hand over her grandmother's. "I'll be respectful, Gigi, but I'm not leaving without some answers."

Gigi nodded; her eyes filled with worry. "I know, my love. Just remember to be gentle in your approach. They have their ways, and you may come across as too strong for their liking."

"I'll be back later. I promise to be careful, and you don't need to worry; I'll watch my words."

As she stormed off the porch, her mind raced with thoughts of Neal and her father, who had kept important aspects of their lives hidden from her. The early fall air was crisp against her skin as she made her way to her car, frustration fueling each step.

Driving up Lawrence County Road into Willow Springs, her mind churned with questions. The quiet, rolling hills that once seemed peaceful now felt like a backdrop to the turmoil raging inside her.

Arriving at the Mercantile in the center of town, Savannah quickly grabbed the items on her list, her thoughts still swirling at her destination. She tried to keep her mind focused on the task at hand, but her mind kept returning to Neal's deception.

As she moved through the market, picking up the items from Gigi's list, she noticed an older man at the checkout counter, struggling to understand the cashier's instructions. The man's frail hands trembled as he fumbled with coins, his face a picture of confusion and embarrassment as he realized he didn't have enough money to cover his purchase.

With a dismissive look, the English cashier spoke impatiently, her tone laced with irritation. "Sir, you don't have enough money for all this. You need to put some items back."

Savannah's annoyance with Neal and her father suddenly found a new target. The young employee's lack of compassion was the final straw. She stepped forward, her voice firm and commanding. "Excuse me, but there's no need to be rude. I'll cover the difference. Add his order to mine."

The cashier's snippy attitude momentarily ceased. "Uh, thank you, ma'am."

Savannah turned to the older man, her voice softening. "It's okay, sir. Let me take care of this for you."

The man looked up; his eyes filled with gratitude. "Thank you, miss. I didn't mean to cause any trouble."

Savannah smiled warmly, handing the cashier a few bills to cover the cost of the groceries. "No trouble at all."

As the older man gathered his groceries, he turned to Savannah, his eyes glistening with unshed tears. "God bless you, young lady. You've shown great kindness today."

Savannah felt a lump in her throat, her anger and frustration momentarily giving way to a sense of fulfillment. "You're very welcome. Take care."

The older gentleman looked fondly at Savannah and even let her carry his groceries to his car. The man's gentle demeanor helped calm Savannah's anxiety as they walked together.

"You're not from around here?" he asked.

"No... not really. I have family here, but I'm from Charleston."

"It's a good place, you know," the man added with a warming smile. "Most folks here are friendly and live simple, honest lives. Except for the occasionally wet behind the ears cashiers," he added with a sly grin. "That's why I chose to live in this mostly Amish community. It's a good place to find some peace."

Savannah nodded, feeling a bit more at ease.

"It certainly seems that way. It's very different from Charleston, no doubt about that."

The man smiled, the creases around his eyes crinkling with warmth. "You'll find the folks around here are always willing to lend a hand or share a kind word. It's a good place to start anew."

Savannah took a deep breath. "Do you know where the Zook farm is?"

The man's face lit up with recognition. "Ah, Harold Zook's farm? Yes, I know it well. It's on Willow Bridge Road. You can get there easily from here."

Just then, a buggy pulled out of the parking lot. The older man pointed to it. "That there is David Zook, Harold's youngest son. Follow him, and he'll lead you to the right place."

Savannah felt a surge of relief. "Thank you so much. You've been very kind."

The man nodded, his smile never wavering. "Safe travels, young lady. I hope you find what you're looking for."

As Savannah watched the buggy turn onto Route 208, she wondered how she would tell one buggy from the next as a row of carriages turned in the same direction. Taking note of the Zook's buggy horse's one-specked leg, she climbed back into her car. The encounter with the older gentleman calmed her nerves and gave her the needed direction.

***

Neal sat quietly in the buggy, waiting for David to return from the market. The trip into town reminded him of the slow-paced life he didn't think he had missed until that moment. While the rhythmic clopping of horse's hooves and the gentle sway of the buggy offered a moment of calm, his thoughts were restless, consumed with Savannah.

As David approached, carrying a small sack of supplies, Neal noticed David's thoughtful expression. David climbed in the buggy, setting the sack between them, and took up the reins. As they started back home, David turned to Neal, a look suggesting something important on his mind.

"You won't believe what I saw at the market," David began. "There was a young English woman, clearly out of her element, but what she did was something else. She stood up for an old man who was short on money, paid for his groceries, and even helped him to his car. Her attitude... it was something to see, nothing like any woman I've ever seen around here."

Neal's mind flashed to Savannah's willingness to help the elderly before he responded, "It's hard not to admire someone who shows that kind of kindness."

David nodded, driving the buggy along the familiar roads. Both stayed quiet for a long time before David cleared his throat and asked, "Why did you choose to marry someone outside our People? Someone so... different from what we know?"

Neal's voice was hoarse and strained with pain as he looked at the passing fields. "I guess I fell in love with her feisty spirit—the complete opposite of the women around here. She had a way of bringing out the best in me."

David snorted. "And how'd that work out for ya?"

"I guess it's more than that. I was running from who I was, from our ways. I thought being with someone like Savannah could help me forget."

David seemed to be gauging his thoughts before replying, "But marrying outside the faith! Especially someone as spirited as you say Savannah is. The whole issue is bound to stir up trouble now that you're back home. How do you think she'll fit in with our family?"

Neal had to admit he'd wondered the same thing. "It may be hard for her to adapt. But hopefully, I can get this sorted out and return to our life in Charleston, and it won't matter much."

David's brow furrowed. "At some point, you'll have to tell her about us."

"*Jah*, I know," Neal replied.

David shook his head as they pulled into the driveway. "I'm not sure an *Englisch* woman would easily fit into all this."

As David guided the buggy down the long, winding driveway toward the barn, he noticed a car following them at a distance. "Looks like we have company," David remarked casually, glancing back through the tiny window at the sleek silver Camry pulling in behind them.

Neal couldn't look right away as his stomach lurched with the possibility of his past catching up with him so soon. Pulling in a deep breath, he turned, and his heart raced as he recognized Savannah's car.

"Stop the buggy!" he shouted, his voice tense.

Sensing his urgency, David nodded and pulled back on the reins, allowing the horse to slow as Neal jumped out.

Neal's eyes locked on Savannah's long, jean-clad legs as she stepped out of the car. His heart nearly jumped out of his chest as he watched her look around with unease and wonder. When she turned toward the buggy, her face reflected anger and disbelief when she saw him.

The sight of her standing there, her fiery eyes searching for answers, sent him into a whirlwind of emotions. He wanted to run to her to hold her and to apologize, but fear of her rejection held him back.

She took a step forward, her voice trembling with fury. "Why didn't you tell me about this?"

Neal stood frozen for a moment, his mind racing. "I... I didn't know how to tell you I had lied about who I was. I was afraid of losing you, afraid you wouldn't understand."

Savannah's eyes flashed with hurt as she closed the distance between them. "You should have trusted me. Do you have any idea how this makes me feel?"

Her hands trembled as she pushed the newspaper article to his chest. "I found out about your Amish background, your family, and everything you never told me. It's like our whole life is nothing but a lie."

Neal took a tentative step closer, his eyes pleading for understanding. "I didn't want to burden you with my past. I wanted to protect you until I figured things out."

Tears welled up in Savannah's eyes, her anger slowly giving way to the pain she'd been carrying. "You don't get to decide what I can handle."

As Neal and Savannah stood face to face, the intensity of their emotions filling the air, the front door of the old farmhouse swung open with a loud creak. Neal's father stepped out onto the porch, his expression stern. "What's all this yelling about?" his voice was gruff and to the point.

Savannah turned to face the aging man, her frustration boiling over. "It's none of your concern!" she shouted back, her composure not bothered by his authoritative stance.

Neal quickly stepped forward, his hand reaching out to touch her arm, his voice in a soothing whisper, "Please, Savannah, that's my father. He's not used to women speaking so forthrightly. It's not our way."

Savannah's eyes flashed with defiance as she took a deep breath, her focus returning to Neal. "I'm here to get answers, and I don't care if my being here upsets your family."

Harold Zook pulled his shoulders back and looked between his son and the *Englisch* woman standing in his driveway. "Neal, who is this? And why is she speaking to you in this manner?"

Neal turned to face his father, hoping to offer him deserved respect. "*Datt, dess is Savannah, mie fraa,*" he replied in *Deitsh.*

His father's eyes widen in disbelief. "Your wife?"

Feeling the tension rise, Savannah took a step closer to Neal, her voice steady but firm. "I'm here to understand why he kept you all hidden from me. We need to have a conversation, and I'm not leaving until we do."

Neal glanced back at his father, said something she didn't understand, then turned his attention back to her. His voice was calm but urgent. "Please keep your voice down some."

Neal sensed his father's words long before he said them. "If she's your wife, she is welcome here. But I expect you to inform her that we do things differently here, and I expect you both to abide by that while on my property."

Neal didn't breathe until he heard the screen door slam behind his father as he returned inside.

Laying his hand gently on Savannah's elbow to direct her away from the house, he spoke in hushed tones. "Please, let's have this conversation somewhere a little more private."

Savannah pulled her arm away, her frustration nearing its end. "I'm not going to be quiet, and I won't stand by and pretend any of this is okay."

"I want to explain, but you'll need to give me some time to sort a few things out first."

"Time!"

"Please, Savannah, quiet," he begged as he guided her away from the car and to the side of the barn.

Replying between clenched teeth, Savannah snarled. "It's been almost a month since we've seen each other, and all you want is more time. Well, we're running out of time. I want answers, and I want them today."

Neal dropped his hands and tried to process Savannah's demand. "I'm sorry I can't explain just yet. But I promise I will, and everything will make sense when I do."

He tried again to reach out to her, but Savannah pulled from his grip and turned on her heels, eyes brimming with tears.

"Savannah, please don't go," he begged. "I did what I felt I had to do… I never meant to hurt you."

She shook her head and pulled in a broken breath. "I need to think. I can't deal with whatever you're hiding from me one more minute." With that, she stormed to her car, her frustration evident in every step.

Neal stood frozen, his heart aching as he watched her drive away, dust kicking up from the tires as she sped down the driveway. The sight of her retreating car left him feeling helpless and uncertain about their future.

David's uneven gait halted beside him as he muttered, "The truth."

CHAPTER 6

Savannah found herself driving along the back roads of Willow Springs, the serene countryside offering a slight reprieve from her confrontation with Neal. She gripped the steering wheel tightly, her mind a whirlwind of thoughts.

Uncertain of her next move and not quite ready to face her grandmother to confess how rude she'd been to Neal's father. Her actions made her wince, and she needed time to relax and gather her thoughts. As she drove, her Amish friend Sarah Byler popped into her mind. She hadn't seen Sarah in a few years but remembered her as a calming presence, someone who always seemed to know the right things to say.

She fondly remembered the last time they had visited. Her life with Neal was in turmoil and the few days she'd spent with her gave her a new outlook on their relationship.

Pulling to a stop alongside the road, Savannah typed Sarah's street name into her GPS. "Please, be home," she whispered as she pulled back onto the blacktop.

The drive to Sarah's house took her deeper into Amish country, and she often had to slow down and maneuver around a buggy or two. Memories of her first encounter with Sarah drifted into her mind, bringing a faint smile to her lips. Her car had broken down near her home, and the kind Amish woman had welcomed her, offering tea and comfort while they waited for help. They had exchanged letters occasionally, but life had pulled them in different directions, and their friendship had become more of a distant connection, but in that moment, she yearned for the closeness they once shared.

As she turned onto the final stretch of road, Savannah spotted Byler's Handmade Furniture sign and Sarah's modest farmhouse near the back of the property. The sight of the picturesque home brought relief, and she felt her tense muscles begin to relax.

Pulling into the driveway, she stepped out of the car; the crisp early autumn air filling her lungs as she walked up to the front door, her steps hesitant but hopeful.

Before she could knock, Sarah had opened the door with a welcoming smile. "Savannah, what on earth brings you back to Willow Springs? The last time I spoke to your grandmother, she said you still lived in Charleston."

Savannah felt a surge of emotions at seeing Sarah's sweet face. "Sarah, it's good to see you too. I hope I'm not intruding."

"Not at all. I've been canning tomatoes and could use a break." Sarah stepped aside and waved her inside.

Savannah followed Sarah to her cozy kitchen. The aroma of simmering tomato sauce and herbs filled the air as she sat at the oak table. Her eyes roamed over the simple yet inviting surroundings.

Sarah busied herself by pouring cold tea into two glasses. "What brings you to Willow Springs? It's been years since we've seen each other."

Savannah sipped the minty sweet tea, the cool, refreshing drink calming her frayed nerves momentarily. "I learned some things about my husband—things he kept from me about his past, his family... he's Amish, Sarah. I had no idea."

Sarah tipped her chin in Savannah's direction with questioning concern etched over her brow. "Amish?"

"Yes… and from this community. I've been visiting my grandmother's home for years, and I never knew his family was from right here in Willow Springs."

"Oh my," Sarah whispered. "Carmichael isn't a typical Amish surname?"

Savannah's eyes filled with tears, her voice trembling, "I guess not, but that's all I've ever known him by." Savannah sighed. "But it gets worse. I confronted him at his family's farm, and it didn't go well. I was rude to his father… and I just… couldn't handle all the emotions."

Savannah stopped to accept a tissue from Sarah and wiped her nose before continuing. "I don't even know who he really is. I feel so lost."

Sarah smiled softly. "You're not lost. You're on a journey, and sometimes the path is difficult and unclear."

The two women sat silently for a few seconds before Sarah asked, "Tell me more about Neal's family. What have you learned so far?"

Savannah sighed, her fingers tracing the rim of her glass. "I found out his real name is Neal Zook."

Sarah's face reflected a disturbing shade of recognition at the mention of his name. She quickly masked her reaction. But not before Savannah noticed the subtle change.

"Sarah," Savannah pressed on, "do you know something about Neal? I'd appreciate it if you know anything to help me understand what's happening."

Sarah hesitated, her eyes shifting slightly as she searched for the right words. "It's not my place to share Neal's story. There are things about his past that only he can tell."

Savannah's frustration grew, her voice rising slightly. "But why, Sarah? What are you not telling me?"

"This is a deeply personal and painful part of Neal's life. It's not my story to tell." Sarah tenderly replied.

Savannah clenched her hands around her glass, her anxiety evident by the tone of her voice. "I just want to know what could have been so bad that he created a whole new life for himself."

Sarah's eyes held a gentle firmness as she spoke. "Trust that Neal will tell you when he's ready. Pressuring him to talk about it before he's ready might only cause more pain."

***

Savannah settled back into her car just as the afternoon sun descended. The drive back from Sarah's did little to calm her, and she entered Gigi's house with a heavy heart.

Sensing her gloomy mood, Gigi looked up from her crocheting with concern. "My dear, you look more unsettled than when you left."

Savannah sank into the worn armchair across from her grandmother, her voice shaky as she recounted her visit with Neal and Sarah.

Gigi reached out, taking Savannah's hands in hers. "The ways of the Amish are much different from the English. They handle conflict calmly and with grace."

Savannah looked at her grandmother's tender eyes and sensed she had something else she needed to say. "And dear, this is one aspect of your husband's life you'll need to embrace."

"How so?" Savannah asked.

Gigi's tone turned soft and assuring. "Respect and calmness are deeply ingrained in their ways. At some point... when he's ready, he'll come and ask for forgiveness, but not until he's ready to forgive himself."

Savannah's curiosity was piqued, and she pressed her grandmother for more information. "What do you know, Gigi?"

Her grandmother only smiled and nodded with a knowing sureness. After a brief silence, she continued in a casual tone, but her expression was thoughtful. "I know he was involved in something that brought great sorrow to this community. And that alone left a shadow over his past. But as far as knowing exactly what happened, I don't."

Gigi squeezed her hand reassuringly. "Patience, my dear. Give him the time he needs to open up, and when he does, listen with an open heart."

"But what am I supposed to do in the meantime? Just sit here and wait for him to get his life together?"

Her grandmother smiled. "I thought you would help me fix this old place up?"

Savannah smiled a genuine grin as she shook her head. "I can do that, starting first thing tomorrow."

***

After Savannah left, the tension in the air lingered like a heavy storm cloud. David returned to work, and Neal's frustration was evident in his every move. Trying to shake off the emotional turmoil, he decided to head to the end of the driveway to fix a broken fence. The physical labor would help clear his head, even while Savannah's visit left an overwhelming sense of dread piercing his heart. He wanted to chase after her, but he wasn't ready to face her just yet.

Just as he hammered the last fence staple in the treated fence post, his phone buzzed against his thigh. Hoping it was Savannah, he pulled it out, only to see a familiar name flash on the screen—Marcus, a former colleague from Charleston. With a new wave of fear, he answered the call.

"Marcus, what's up?"

"Neal, you need to listen to me," his friend demanded. "I just heard that they've called in the authorities and are out to find you and bring you in for questioning. Whatever documents you submitted for that government contract stirred up a lot of trouble for all of us. Look, I've got to go, but I wanted to give you a heads up."

Neal stood and stared at the now blank screen, his mind racing. Just then, a car pulled into the driveway, catching Neal's attention. His heart pounded as the vehicle approached. Two men dressed in dark suits stepped out, their expressions unreadable.

"Neal Zook?" one asked, holding up a governmental badge. "We need you to come with us."

Neal's stomach dropped. "What's this about?" As if he didn't already know.

"We're with the defense department, and we'd like to ask you some questions about Neal Carmicheal," the man said firmly. "Please, come with us."

Neal's mind raced, thinking of Savannah and the unresolved mess he'd created. He nodded slowly as he climbed in, accidentally dropping his phone on the ground, but there was no time to retrieve it.

Pulling away, Neal looked back at his parents' house, full of fear and regret. How would he save himself from the chaos he'd put himself in? He closed his eyes, whispering a silent prayer. "Please, Lord, help me find a way out of this and let Savannah find it in her heart to forgive me when it's all over."

***

Savannah had resolved to give Neal the needed space, focusing instead on helping her Gigi around the house. The days were filled with the scent of pine cleaner and fresh paint, the satisfaction of fixing what she could. She felt a sense of purpose at seeing the joy on her grandmother's face with each completed project.

She was up on a ladder, cleaning the gutters, when she heard a car pull into the driveway behind her. She looked down to see her father, Chad's black truck. His voice bellowed toward her out his open window.

"Savannah Mae, get off that ladder. What are you doing up there?"

She whined. "What does it look like I'm doing?"

"You shouldn't be doing that alone. Someone needs to be holding the ladder. You could get hurt," he demanded as he stepped closer.

Savannah climbed down the ladder. "Someone needs to take care of the place, and you've shown no interest in caring for it. Besides, I can handle it. I've been handling everything on my own for a long time now, if I remember correctly."

Savannah watched the familiar color rise to her father's cheeks as he waited for her to finish. "I know… the same old story… I was never there for you speech. Come on, Savannah, isn't it time we get past all that?"

She crossed her arms. "It wasn't just you… it was both you and Mom I couldn't count on. Do you have any idea what that did to me?"

Her father took a deep breath, his eyes filling with regret. "Look, I don't know how many times I can apologize for how I handled things when you were little, and I'm sorry you feel I wasn't there for you. Hopefully, someday, you'll figure out that being a parent doesn't come with an owner's manual, and I did the best I could with what I knew."

Savannah felt her voice turn cold, and she couldn't stop the words before they spilled out of her mouth. "I had to learn to take care of myself because you were too wrapped up in your own issues to see I was hurting too."

Her father's shoulders slumped, but he tried to lighten the mood by stepping closer and wrapping his arm around her shoulders. "Come now… can't we put that behind us for now?" He took a finger and prodded her side. "I promise not to poke the bear too much."

She twisted away from his apologetic embrace, her anger giving way to tears as she remembered his addictive past. "You just can't waltz back into my life and pretend everything is okay."

"No, I can't, but I can try to make amends. I know I failed you when you needed me the most, but I can't change the past, no matter how hard I try. Someday, I hope you'll find it in your heart to forgive me."

Savannah's heart ached as she watched the sincerity in his eyes melt some of her pain away. She fought the tears misting her eyes. "I've got too many other things on my mind right now to even consider working through our past."

Helping him carry the ladder back to the side of the house, Savannah couldn't help but chastise herself for being so hard on him. She wanted a healthy relationship with both of her parents, but never felt she could let her guard down low enough to let either of them get too close. The pain of her childhood left a long-lasting bitter taste in her mouth.

"Have you talked to your mother lately?"

Before she could answer her father's question, Gigi stepped out on the porch, calming the storm beginning to rage within her. A pain twinged in her chest at just how much she missed her mother. Their few and far-between conversations always ended in battle, so she avoided the war as best she could. But deep inside, she missed what they used to have before divorce, before addiction, and before broken promises tore her family apart.

As the three stood on the porch, the tension began to ease with Gigi's welcoming embrace around her son. "What a pleasant surprise. Two of my favorite people visiting me at the same time. What's a woman to do with such overwhelming joy?" she exclaimed.

That evening, they gathered in the living room. The flickering fireplace took the chill off the drafty room, and Savannah suddenly relaxed from the ongoing tension with Neal.

Gigi, ever the peacemaker, started the conversation with a warm smile. "It's good to have you here, Chad. I've missed you."

Chad returned her smile, his eyes reflecting a new calmness. Gone were the shifty eyes and nervous energy of the past. "I've missed being here too, Mom. There's something about this old place that's comforting."

Listening to her father and Gigi talk, Savannah couldn't help but notice that there was something different about her father. A peace about him that she'd never witnessed before. He seemed more sure of himself, more centered. Savannah studied her father briefly before adding, "You seem different, Dad... what changed?"

Her father looked over at her and smiled. "A lot has changed, Savannah. I realized I needed to make some serious changes in my life. I couldn't keep running from my problems."

Gigi nodded, her eyes shining with pride. "Your father's been on quite a journey, dear. It's been a blessing to see him find his way."

Savannah watched her father sit up straighter before he replied, "I've found something that's helped me make sense of my past and find a path forward. It's given me a sense of peace and purpose that I never had before."

Savannah raised an eyebrow, hoping the hint of skepticism running through her head would dampen his spirit.

Her father glanced at Gigi, who gave him an encouraging nod. He turned back to Savannah. "I'm clean and determined to make things up to you and your grandmother."

Savannah's mind raced with conflicting thoughts. She wanted to believe him, but years of disappointment had built a wall around her heart. "You've said things before, Dad. You made promises you couldn't keep and claimed you've changed.

Why should this be any different?" She couldn't help but notice how her words affected her father's composure.

"I know I've let you down before... and I have a lot to make up for, but I'm committed to proving it through my actions, not just words."

The sincerity in his voice gave her reason to pause, and she felt her defenses begin to waver. Surely, she wouldn't let him know that.

Taking the opportunity to change the subject, Gigi began to share stories of her Amish past. "Now that you know about my past, let me explain a few things."

Savannah was quick to jump in, aiming her comment at her father. "Yeah... Dad, thanks for never telling me we have Amish blood running through our veins. That should have been something someone shared with me before now."

"I guess I never saw it as a bloodline thing since being Amish is a way of life."

"Still, I think it would have been nice to know."

"Now, now... Savannah, calm down. Let me explain so there's no doubt why you weren't told the truth," Gigi exclaimed.

"I wasn't always outside the Amish community," Gigi admitted. "I grew up about thirty miles north of here in a small Amish settlement, much like Willow Springs. Life was simple, full of hard work as well as lots of challenges."

Savannah listened intently. "Why did you leave? What made you decide to step away from that life?"

Gigi sighed; her smile tinged with sadness. "It wasn't an easy decision, my dear. I fell in love with your grandfather, who wasn't Amish or from our community. I had to choose between my family and my heart—I chose love."

Savannah crossed her legs and took a sip of tea before asking, "Was the challenge because you wanted to leave?"

A solemn look creased her grandmother's forehead before she answered. "Life has a way of challenging us, making us face difficult choices. But those choices shape who we are, and they become part of our testimony."

Savannah's heart softened as she listened to her grandmother relive a part of her past she had buried long ago.

"My father was the district bishop and demanded his family to follow very high standards." Gigi giggled before continuing.

"When I met your grandfather, I fell hard for his boyish charm. He worked for my *datt*, and I found every excuse in the book to be where he was. It took my family a couple of years to catch on to us, but by then, it was too late. We were in love and the only way we could be together is if I left the confines of both my Amish family and the community that had molded me." Gigi got a starry far-off look in her eyes, before she said, "You wouldn't know it now, but there was a time in my life when I had a pretty defiant streak... much like someone else I know."

Savannah laughed. "I find that hard to believe."

Her father added a throaty grunt. "Gigi isn't anything like she was when your Aunt Lala and I were growing up." He rubbed the back of his upper arm. "There was more than one occasion when her fingers would gently squeeze me into submission."

Her grandmother's face turned a shade of pink before she replied, "We all make mistakes when it comes to raising children, but we do the best we can. In the end, we pray our mistakes don't make a lasting impact."

"What kind of mistakes did you make, Gigi?"

Her grandmother laughed. "Oh, child, too many to count."

Savannah turned to her father. "And you, Dad? Why did you leave Willow Springs?"

Her father took a deep breath, his facial expression pained. "I, too, fell in love with someone off-limits. She was Amish, and our relationship would have never been accepted. I knew what my mother had gone through as a child, and I never wanted that for my friend. I joined the service to give her a chance to live the life she was meant to lead without the complications I would bring."

Savannah glanced at her father, noticing the gentleness in his eyes, a gentleness she cherished in Neal's personality. It struck her that the trait she admired in Neal was reflected in her father as well.

Intrigued by the look of wishfulness on her father's face, Savannah inquired, "Tell me about her. What was she like?"

Her father took a few minutes to answer. "She was like a wounded puppy when I first met her. She was working at her father's bakery when I first saw her. I remember the day like it was yesterday."

Savannah couldn't help but smile as he relived what seemed like happier days.

"Her name was Nelly, and the first couple of times she waited on me, she couldn't even look me in the eye, but eventually, I was able to get her to open up enough to at least offer me a greeting. She was guarded and quiet when her father was around, and it wasn't until later that I learned she had an unhealthy fear of him."

As the evening wore on, Savannah couldn't deny the joy of having her father around, and she felt herself warming to his presence.

Tracy Fredrychowski

CHAPTER 7

After a few days of working at Gigi's house and catching up with her father, Savannah felt more equipped to face Neal again. Determined to get some answers, she drove to the Zook farm, her heart pounding as she crept closer. She hoped Neal would be outside and she wouldn't have to approach the house, but as she pulled into the driveway, Neal was nowhere to be seen. Instead, his brother met her with a stern expression.

Savannah stepped out of the car just as David walked toward her. "I need to see Neal. Is he around?"

David crossed his arms, the frustration evident in his stance. "He's gone. Disappeared again."

Savannah's heart sank. "What do you mean he's gone? Where did he go?"

David shook his head, irritation evident in his tone. "I don't know. He just got up and left, the same as before. He left us all hanging, scrambling for answers once again."

Savannah fought the rise of angry tears brimming her bottom lashes. "I don't understand why he keeps running. Please help me understand."

David studied her for a moment, let out a short snort, and said, "Come inside. Maybe it's time you heard the whole story."

Savannah looked at her car and then toward the house. Did she dare look for answers in his family? In the end, she nodded and followed him to the house.

David slowed his steps. "By the way, I'm David, Neal's younger brother."

"I'm sorry, David. I wish we were meeting under better circumstances."

"*Jah*, me too."

Savannah whispered as they headed up the stairs. "I didn't give your father a good first impression the other day. Are you sure he'll talk to me?"

"Oh, don't worry about him. His bark is much bigger than his bite."

Savannah snickered as David pulled open the squeaking screen door at the side of the house, which led into the spacious kitchen. As they walked in, the lingering smells of breakfast were still heavy in the air. Neal's parents were sitting at a large pine table, their faces etched with surprise at her presence. David gestured for her to sit, and they joined them at the table.

David started; his voice steady as he addressed his parents. "Savannah came looking for Neal." He paused long enough for his father to put down his coffee cup and his mother to get comfortable with Savannah. "I think she deserves to hear the truth behind Neal's odd behavior."

Savannah sat, twisting her hands on her lap as she took in the surroundings. The Zook home reflected cleanliness and order, a trait that Neal exemplified without fault. Void of pictures or excessive knick-knacks, the simple surroundings gave her reason to relax.

Neal's father, Harold, looked at Savannah, his expression stern but not unkind. "Before we begin, I must address your behavior the other day. We don't handle conflict in that manner. Our community believes in speaking respectfully and resolving differences calmly, and I expect you to honor our traditions while you're here."

Savannah felt a flush of embarrassment and regret. She looked down at her hands and then back up at Harold. "I'm really sorry, Mr. Zook. I know I was out of line. I have a lot to learn about the Amish ways, and I shouldn't have been so rude. My grandmother warned me, but I didn't listen to her advice. Please accept my apology."

Harold's face relaxed. "Apology accepted. We all make mistakes, and how we learn from them is what matters."

Harold leaned forward, his eyes curious. "Who's your grandmother? Are you staying in Willow Springs?"

Savannah nodded, grateful for the shift in conversation. "My grandmother, Brenda Fisher, lives on Lawrence County Road near the Apple Blossom Inn."

Harold's eyes lit up with recognition. "Brenda is quite an asset to this community. If I remember correctly, she has ties to the Amish herself."

Savannah nodded. "Yes, she does, and I just found out about those ties the other day. I was pretty surprised to hear she grew up much like Neal has."

Priscilla smiled warmly. "Mrs. Fisher has always been a bridge between our community and the outside world. She understands our ways and has always been the first to explain things to those who often ask too many questions."

Savannah felt a sense of pride for her grandmother. "She's been amazing to me. Staying with her has been an eye-opener. I'm learning so much."

Priscilla furrowed her brow and looked long and hard at Savannah. "Did you meet Neal here in Willow Springs?"

Savannah chuckled. "Heavens no. We met in Charleston."

The older woman swayed her head from side to side and mumbled something she didn't understand in Pennsylvania Dutch.

Harold replied harshly to his wife's comment in the same language before they turned their attention back to her, nodding approvingly. "You're in good hands. She'll help you understand our ways."

David glared at his mother before cutting in. "It's time Savannah learns the truth."

Harold leaned back in his chair, resting his hands on the arms of the chair. "Neal's been carrying a heavy burden for years. It all started as a harmless prank that went terribly wrong. He and some other boys decided to take three younger boys into the woods to teach them survival techniques. They thought it would be fun, but they went too deep into the woods, and the boys got lost on a night where the temperatures dipped in the single digits."

Savannah listened intently, her heart aching for the young Neal who had made such a tragic mistake.

David continued; his voice strained under the memories. "The three boys ended up freezing to death that night. Neal went home and slept, thinking they'd find their way out, even in the severe weather conditions. When they were finally found two days later, it was too late. Neal was overwhelmed with guilt and shame. He hid that he had anything to do with it for weeks before he up and left without so much as a goodbye."

Neal's mother, brimming with tears, added softly, "When the truth finally came out, he couldn't face what he had done, so he ran. That was the last we'd seen of him until last week."

Savannah could hardly control the pain in her heart as Neal's family relived the drama that forced Neal from his home. "I had no idea. He never shared any of this with me."

Neal's father spoke up. "He was ashamed of what he did and the secret he kept. He thought running away would make forgetting easier, but it only worsened things."

Savannah felt a deep compassion for her husband, her anger softening. "We need to find him."

David snorted. "Good luck with that. When he doesn't want to be found... ain't no one gonna find him."

With a small catch of breath, Priscilla added, "It's time he faced his past and found some peace."

As they sat around the table, she finally understood the mystery behind her husband's dark eyes.

She tried to absorb Neal's internal struggles and the reason behind his actions, but it still didn't explain why he felt he couldn't come to her and share his struggles.

With the support of Neal's family, Savannah set out to find him. They contacted friends and community members, spreading the word that Neal was missing and needed to come home. Savannah felt a growing bond with the Zook family, and their shared mission brought them closer.

With each passing day, Savannah's heart ached deeper with the thought he might never return home.

***

Neal sat on the cold bench in his cell, staring at the walls. The gray concrete walls seemed to close in on him, a harsh reminder of the lies he had built his life upon; he faced the consequences of his actions. Officials had caught up with the false identity he crafted, and he was now serving a thirty-day misdemeanor charge.

He had decided not to contact Savannah or his family. The shame was too much to bear. How could he face them knowing the depth of his deceit? Instead, he chose to suffer alone, hoping that the time of reflection would lead to some redemption.

The days passed slowly, each one blending into the next. Meals were a blur, and conversations with other inmates were sparse. Neal spent most of his time in silence, contemplating the choices that had led him there.

Looking for some reprieve from the dark, dreary common area, he found himself in the dimly lit chapel when something shifted within him. The chapel was the only place he found quiet. As he stared at the simple wooden cross at the front of the room, memories of his Amish upbringing flooded. The values of honesty, humility, and community he once cherished now seemed like distant echoes. He had strayed so far from the path, and the realization hit him hard.

A prison minister entered the room, a kind-faced man with a gentle demeanor. He approached Neal, sitting beside him without saying a word. After a few moments of silence, the darkly dressed Mennonite minister spoke. "Is there something pressing on your heart, son?"

Neal sighed before he spoke. "I've made so many mistakes. I don't even recognize myself anymore."

The man nodded; his eyes full of understanding. "Have you sought forgiveness?"

Neal shook his head, tears welling in his eyes. "I don't even know where to start."

The older gentleman stood, waited a few seconds, and added, "Seek strength in your faith and let it guide you back to the person you want to be."

Neal closed his eyes, the minister's words sinking deep into his soul. He hadn't prayed in a long time, but now, in this quiet moment, he reached out to the Lord.

"Lord, I don't know if I deserve forgiveness, but I need it. Help me find my way back to the man I once was. Give me the strength to make amends and the courage to face those I've hurt."

In the following days, Neal immersed himself in one of the Bibles he found in the book cart. He began to see his incarceration not as a sentence but as a period of awakening… a way for *Gott* to break his will. He reflected on the values he had abandoned and made a silent vow to reclaim them.

As he lay on the thin mattress at night, thoughts of Savannah occupied his mind. He missed her fiercely but knew he couldn't contact her until he was ready to face her with honesty and humility. He needed to make things right within himself first.

***

Unable to locate Neal, Savannah struggled to find purpose and focused on building a life in Willow Springs. Not ready to give up on the chance he'd return, she began looking for a job.

While visiting her friend Sarah, she heard about an opportunity. "You know, Savannah," Sarah said thoughtfully as they sipped tea on the porch, "the Apple Blossom Inn is hiring. I hear Mrs. Sorensen is looking for an event planner. It might be a good fit for you."

"Really? That sounds promising. But… what is Mrs. Sorensen like?"

Sarah chuckled. "I've never worked for her, but the girls in the community claim she can be tough. She doesn't tolerate nonsense but is fair and appreciates hard work."

***

Savannah mustered enough courage to walk across the street to the Apple Blossom Inn the next day. The charming bed-and-breakfast stood amidst a row of apple trees, whose leaves were whirling to the ground in the crisp autumn breeze.

Stepping inside, Savannah was greeted by a warm and inviting atmosphere. The polished floors, antique staircase, and the scent of freshly baked apple pie lingered in the air. She approached the front desk, where Mrs. Sorensen, a stern-looking woman in her late sixties, was sorting through some papers.

"Excuse me, Mrs. Sorensen?" Savannah began.

"I'm Savannah Carmichael... Savannah Zook."

"Well, what is it?" The older woman snapped, "Carmichael or Zook?"

"Carmichael," she muttered. "I heard you were looking for an event planner, and I'd like to apply for the position."

Mrs. Sorensen looked up, her dark eyes scanning Savannah from head to toe. "I see," she exclaimed over her wire-rimmed glasses, which she wore low on her nose. "What makes you think you're qualified for the job?"

Savannah took a deep breath. "I have experience in event planning from my previous job in Charleston. I've managed high-profile events and have a keen eye for detail. I believe I could bring a lot to the table."

Mrs. Sorensen raised an eyebrow. "Charleston, you say? That's a far cry from Willow Springs. Why are you here?"

Savannah hesitated, then decided on honesty. "I'm staying with my grandmother. I needed a change, and my husband's family is from this area."

Mrs. Sorensen nodded slowly, considering Savannah's words. "Well, event planning here is different. Our guests are mostly Amish and those interested in the Amish way of life. I typically like my employees to have a working knowledge of the area and the Amish lifestyle."

Mrs. Sorensen went back to her paperwork. "This position will take more than a working knowledge of event planning. I need someone who has lived among the People or has an Amish background." She looked up over her glasses and gave

Savannah a disapproving once-over. "I can clearly see you have neither."

Suddenly embarrassed for her inappropriate attire, Savannah tried to compose herself into a well-meant, spirited rebuttal. "If you don't mind me asking, how long would I have to learn such things before you needed to fill the position?"

The older woman let out a sarcastic grunt. "I'm in no hurry, but I doubt you could learn such things in such a short amount of time. Living and working like the Amish are embedded in a person from the time they're knee high to a grasshopper."

"I'm a quick learner, and I can only bet you won't come across someone with my credentials here in Willow Springs. Will you take a chance on me and give me at least a month to engross myself in the Amish community?"

Something about the stoic older woman raising her chin let Savannah know she had piqued her curiosity. "A month, you say? And how will I know you've learned enough to be able to tend to our guests with the ease and grace of a well-mannered Amish woman?"

Savannah thought long and hard about Mrs. Sorensen's question. *That might be hard to pull off for even me, she thought*. But she surely wasn't going to let the challenge scare her away. "I find the prospect enticing."

"You'll need to learn the customs and traditions to make them feel at home. You think you can do that in a month?" the older woman was quick to ask.

"If it means you'll wait and give me a chance, I'll give it my all."

Mrs. Sorensen looked up. "One more thing. I require all my staff to wear traditional Amish clothing to maintain the inn's authentic appeal. That might be one more hurdle you'll have to grasp."

Savannah hesitated, the idea of wearing Amish clothes unsettling, but she needed this job. "Yes, ma'am, that won't be a problem."

Savannah could tell by the slight twitch of the woman's upper lip that she didn't believe she had the strength to do what was required.

"Remember, respect and understanding are the key here. I won't tolerate anything less."

Savannah gave the woman a date and promised to return to prove she was the right person for the job. As she left the inn, her heart felt lighter. Despite the unconventional dress code and the challenge of adapting to a new way of life, she felt a new surge of hope. The job at the Apple Blossom Inn wasn't just a job; it was a chance to learn about Neal's and Gigi's Amish past.

***

Walking across the street to Gigi's home, Savannah found her grandmother digging potatoes in the garden. The earthy scent of freshly turned soil filled the air, mingling with the crispness of fall. Gigi looked up, a warm smile spreading about her face as Savannah approached. "Did you get the job?" Gigi asked as she brushed dirt from her hands.

Savannah knelt to add the freshly turned red potatoes to the waiting bushel basket. "Possibly. She will hold the job for me for thirty days until I can learn everything I can about the Amish way of life."

Gigi chuckled with amusement. "And how do you expect to do that?"

Savannah's brow furrowed. "I haven't quite figured that out just yet."

Gigi leaned on her shovel, giving much thought to Mrs. Sorensen's requirements. "The only way you're truly going to learn is by living like the Amish. You need to stay in an Amish house, work on a farm, and embrace their daily life. It's the best way to grasp their culture, faith, and family life."

"You can't be serious," Savannah gasped. "I was hoping you could teach me what I need to know."

"Oh, child, I may live close to the land, but I've spent more of my life as an *Englisher* than I ever did Amish."

Savannah fell back on her heels and waited for her grandmother to unearth another scoop of potatoes. Live with an Amish family? "I like a challenge, but I'm not sure I'm up for that."

Gigi flashed her a smile. "It's the only way you'll truly understand. It will be an adjustment for sure."

Savannah sighed in frustration. "What have I gotten myself into, Gigi?"

Her grandmother chuckled, a glint of mischievous in her eyes. "Oh, I know you can do anything if you want it bad enough, and the minute I say you can't, you'll prove to me that you can."

Later that evening, as they sat around the dinner table, the conversation turned to Savannah's new job and the prospect of her living with an Amish family. Her father looked skeptical as he took a bite of stew. "So, you're really going to give up your makeup, phone, and lifestyle to live like the Amish?"

"Yes, Dad. I'm serious about this. I need to understand their way of life if I'm going to do my job properly."

Chad laughed, shaking his head. "I just can't picture it."

Savannah glanced at her father, her eyes flashing with determination. "I know you don't think I can do this, but I need to, not just for the job, but for myself. I must understand Neal's world; this is the only way."

Gigi wiped her mouth and asked, "What about Neal's folks? There might be no better way to understand your new family than living with them for a while."

Savannah set her fork aside. "My thoughts exactly."

CHAPTER 8

Inside, Harold and Priscilla were enjoying a quiet evening at the kitchen table. Priscilla's brow furrowed with worry as Harold's calm demeanor stayed steady.

"Harold, I still can't believe Neal disappeared again. What are we going to do if he doesn't come back? And, for that matter, what is Savannah going to do?"

"We must have faith that he will find his way home in his own time."

Before Priscilla could respond, there was a knock at the door. They exchanged puzzled glances before Harold moved to the front room. Opening the door, Harold was surprised to see Savannah standing there, looking nervous. "Savannah?"

"Mr. Zook, I... I've come to ask you a favor."

Harold looked out at her car, hoping to see her grandmother. "Is everything alright with your grandmother?"

Savannah stumbled with an answer. "Yes, she's fine. She just can't help me understand your way of life like you and your wife can." She paused, hoping to gauge a favorable response on his weathered face. "It was actually her idea for me to come here and ask to stay with you for a while."

"Ain't so?" he replied, running a quick hand through his hair and looking back toward the kitchen. "Wait here for a moment." The door shut as quickly as it opened, leaving Savannah alone on the porch.

"What is it, Harold?" Priscilla asked, sensing something unusual.

"It's Savannah. She's asking to stay with us. She wants to learn about our way of life."

Priscilla's tone turned sharp. "Stay with us? Why on earth would she want to do that?"

Harold rubbed the back of his neck. "I'm not totally clear about her reasoning."

Priscilla frowned. "Having her underfoot could be disruptive."

Harold nodded. "I know, but she's family, and maybe this is an opportunity for us to get to know her."

With a gesture of resignation, Priscilla looked out the window. "Alright, if you think it's the right thing to do, we'll try it. But she'll need to follow our rules and respect our customs."

Harold placed a reassuring hand on her shoulder. "I'll make sure she understands."

Harold returned to the door, opening it more welcomingly this time. "Yes, you can stay. But you'll need to respect our ways in all things." He pointed at the holes in the legs of her jeans. "You'll need to start with your attire."

Savannah nodded eagerly, relief washing over her at his response. "Yes, sir, I promise to do my best to respect all aspects of your life here."

Harold stepped aside to let her in. Entering the kitchen, Savannah couldn't help but notice the apprehensive look etched on Priscilla's face. The next few weeks were going to be a challenge. But she was determined to win Neal's mother over the best she could.

Mrs. Zook led her to a small room upstairs at the end of the hall. "This will be your room. You can unpack and settle in. Dinner will be ready in about thirty minutes."

"Thank you, Mrs. Zook. I really appreciate this."

"Call me Priscilla, and you can thank Harold. I'm not so certain this is a good idea."

After Priscilla had left, Savannah looked around the room. It was simple but cozy, with handmade quilts and a view of the sprawling wheat fields outside. Looking down at her clothes, she wished she had thought to pack something more conservative.

Downstairs, Harold and Priscilla resumed their conversation, this time with a sense of cautious optimism.

"She's going to have a tough time adjusting," Priscilla said, taking a casserole from the oven. "But maybe it's exactly what she needs to help Neal, should he ever return."

Harold nodded with a thoughtful look etched across his brow. "Sometimes, it takes stepping into someone else's shoes to understand them."

Priscilla giggled. "Well, she'll get a feel for that when I dig out some of the girls' old sneakers and work dresses after supper."

The savory smells of supper swayed upstairs, and Savannah's stomach growled at the aroma. Thirty minutes later, she found herself seated at the table, the soft glow of the oil lamp adding just enough light to the kitchen.

Without warning, Harold bowed his head, and Priscilla followed suit. Savannah, unsure of what to do, quickly lowered her head. She kept her eyes closed, waiting for someone to speak, but all she heard was the rustling of fabric, the clink of glass, and the gentle tick of the clock on the wall. The silence stretched on, and Savannah began to feel uncomfortable.

After an eternity, she opened her eyes slightly and peeked around. Neal's parents were both looking at her with slight smiles on their lips. Savannah felt a blush of embarrassment creeping up her cheeks.

Harold cleared his throat and explained. "We say our prayers quietly. I usually tap my glass when we're finished.

Savannah nodded. "Thank you for explaining. I wasn't sure how long to keep my head down."

Priscilla quietly added, "It's not how long you keep your head down; the conversation you have with the Lord is what matters most."

Harold and Priscilla had a light conversation, asking Savannah about her life in Charleston and her family. She answered politely, feeling more at ease with each passing moment. As they talked, Savannah couldn't help but notice the calm and peaceful atmosphere of the Zook home. And for a split second, she understood her husband's disposition more than ever. He hadn't grown up in a stressful, high-tension environment. Everything about his family life was summarized in the peace and serenity she felt at that exact moment.

After dinner, Savannah helped Mrs. Zook with the dishes. The warm water and simple tasks were a welcome distraction from her swirling thoughts. When the last dish was dried and put away, Priscilla turned to her and said, "Come with me," leading her back upstairs.

They stopped at the first bedroom at the top of the stairs, and Priscilla started to rummage around in an old trunk at the end of the bed. She handed her a stack of folded dresses and aprons. "These are some of my daughter's old things she left behind once she married and moved away. They should fit you fine."

Savannah looked at the plain clothes, already feeling a twinge of discomfort. This was made worse when Priscilla handed her a few pairs of black stockings and a well-worn pair of black sneakers.

"We're known as plain people," Priscilla explained. "This refers to our dress. We seek to avoid bright, flashy, attention-seeking colors. We aim to cover up the body and not draw attention to ourselves. Our plain dress allows us to speak of God without using words."

Savannah tried to speak without revealing the turmoil she was experiencing inside. "So, you're saying I have to wear these... plain clothes?"

Priscilla's eyes tightened a bit. "Yes. While you're staying here, I expect you to respect our customs. If you want to learn about our way of life, you must immerse yourself in every aspect. That includes dressing properly so what we wear doesn't bring attention to our bodies."

Savannah bristled. "I don't see why what I wear should matter so much. Isn't it what's inside that counts?"

"Yes, but our external appearance reflects our inner values. We believe women should dress modestly." Priscilla nodded to Savannah's bangle bracelets, hooped earrings lining her earlobes, and the small diamond chip positioned discreetly on the side of her nose. "We should not adorn ourselves with jewelry and are to have a meek and quiet spirit."

Savannah tried to hold back a gasp. This was the complete opposite of her personality. This would be harder than she thought. She nodded and walked to her room at the end of the hall.

Priscilla continued to talk as Savannah strolled away. "A plain, modest dress with no jewelry or makeup is a witness for Christ without using words."

Savannah felt a simmering frustration toward Neal's mother. The tension between them was unmistakable, but Savannah was determined to prove she could handle it, no matter how difficult it would be.

Standing in the small room, staring at the plain dress and apron on the bed, she picked up the dress and tried to figure out how to put it on. There were no buttons or zippers, just a series of fabric folds. She fumbled with the material, trying to close the bodice as best she could. Her frustration mounted as the dress gaped open, refusing to stay in place.

Giving up, she marched downstairs, holding the dress together. She found Priscilla in the kitchen, preparing some tea.

"Mrs. Zook, I need help," Savannah said, her voice laced with irritation.

Priscilla turned and immediately covered her mouth to stifle a laugh. "Oh, dear, I forgot to explain. Our dresses and aprons are held together with straight pins."

"You can't be serious?" Savannah asked in disbelief.

Priscilla nodded, still smiling. "Here, let me help you."

She stepped forward and carefully pinned the dress closed, showing Savannah how to do it properly. "You see, we use straight pins to avoid the adornment of buttons and zippers," Priscilla explained. "It's all part of our commitment to simplicity and humility."

Savannah watched intently as Priscilla's hands worked, trying to memorize the technique. "This is going to take some getting used to," she admitted.

Priscilla chuckled. "It's not so hard once you get the hang of it. You'll see."

After Priscilla secured the last pin, Savannah tried to move around, feeling the unfamiliar tightness of the pins. "I feel like I'm going to prick myself when I move."

Priscilla laughed. "It takes practice, but you'll get there. Let's look at the apron now."

They worked together to fasten the apron, with Priscilla demonstrating how to fold the pin in securely. Savannah stumbled a few times, but Priscilla's patience and gentle guidance helped ease her frustration.

"There you go," Priscilla said, admiring their work. "You almost look like one of us. We'll work on adding a head covering another day."

Savannah glanced down at herself, feeling a little silly in the old-fashioned clothes that felt strange against her skin. "Thank you, Mrs. Zook."

Savannah joined Harold and Priscilla in the living room as the evening continued. A small fire had been lit in the woodstove to ward off the cool evening, and Harold read from an old German Bible that looked much like the one she had of Neal's.

While she didn't understand the words, something comforting about the cadence of his voice drew her in. Every once in a while, he would stop and explain the meaning of the passage.

His voice was deep and soothing as he translated, in English, *"Wives, submit yourselves unto your husbands, as it is fit in the*

Lord." He paused, looking at Priscilla, who smiled warmly and nodded.

"This verse," Harold explained, "is about harmony and respect that should exist in a marriage. It's not about being above the other, but about mutual respect and love."

Priscilla added, "It means that in our faith, we believe in supporting and respecting each other; it's about love and partnership, not control."

Savannah listened, feeling a pang of guilt. She never really understood these concepts in her own marriage. She had always been so focused on her independence and control that it often caused strife between Neal and her. Absorbing their words, she took in the calm, loving atmosphere. It reminded her of Gigi's home, where love and faith were intertwined daily.

"My grandparents had a marriage like that," Savannah muttered.

"They must have greatly influenced you," Priscilla said.

"They did, especially my Gigi. She's always been there for me, showing me love and patience even when I didn't deserve it."

Harold smiled. "That's the power of faith and love. It can transform us and help us grow. And you're here now, ready to learn and understand, *jah*?"

Savannah felt a tear slip down her cheek. The tenderness with which they spoke to her touched her. "I hope so; I really do."

***

Savannah lay on the narrow bed. She felt like an outsider in the simple, quiet world, so different from hers. In a pensive mood, she pulled her cell phone from her purse, checking it one last time to see if Neal had called or left a message. The battery would die any minute, but she couldn't help but check.

As she scrolled through the last few pictures of her and Neal, she noticed the sadness in his eyes—a hurt or distant pain she couldn't pinpoint until now.

The room was dark, and she fumbled with the oil lamp, eventually giving up. She dressed in the dark, pulling on her familiar comfy nightclothes, happy to take off the thick stockings and scratchy fabric of the Amish dress. She couldn't help but feel out of place, yet there was a strange comfort in the simplicity of her surroundings.

***

Neal sat on the hard cot in his cell, letting the pressure of his actions press down on him. The small window high on the wall allowed a sliver of light to cascade onto the gray concrete walls. His thoughts were a jumble of guilt, regret, and longing to be released from the constant internal battle. As he lay there, the minister's words echoed in his mind, urging him to seek forgiveness and make amends.

The kind and gentle Mennonite minister had spent hours talking with him about his past mistakes. The last time they met, he had encouraged him to write a letter to the bishop of his Old Order community, asking for permission to contact the families of the three boys whose lives were tragically cut short.

Neal picked up his pen, his hand trembling slightly as he put it to the paper. His mind raced with thoughts of the boys, their families, and the pain he had caused. In a spasm of despair, he began to write.

Dear Bishop Weaver,

I hope this letter finds you well and in good health. I'm seeking your guidance and permission in a matter that has burdened my heart for many years.

As you may recall, I was involved in a tragic incident that resulted in the death of three young boys from our community. At the time, I was young, scared, and made poor decisions that led to this devastating outcome. Instead of facing the consequences of my actions, I fled, leaving behind a trail of unanswered questions, pain, and sorrow.

I have spent the last six years in deep regret, which has led me to make more bad decisions that have left me seeking peace. I humbly ask your permission to contact the boys' families to offer my heartfelt apologies and seek reconciliation with my family and the church.

I understand this request may bring back painful memories, and I do not take it lightly. I'm willing to do whatever it takes to make amends and restore the trust I have broken to both my family and the community I left behind.

Thank you for considering my request. I await your guidance and pray for the strength to do what is right.

Neal Zook

Neal read the letter several times, his heart beating with relief and hesitation. He closed his eyes and prayed for the power to face the families, to seek their forgiveness, and to find his way back to the community.

A week later, Neal received a letter back. With unsteady hands, he opened the letter and began to read.

Dear Neal,

I received your letter and have prayed for guidance in responding to your request. The pain and sorrow caused by your past events have left deep scars in our community, but our faith teaches us the importance of forgiveness.

I have spoken with the boys' families, and while it will be a difficult and emotional journey, they have agreed to your request. They understand the importance of reconciliation and are willing to hear your apology.

I will support you on this journey, but you must prove your sincerity through your actions.

May God guide you on this path and grant you the strength to face the challenges ahead.

In faith and fellowship,

Bishop Mose Weaver

Neal read the letter several times. The bishop's words gave him hope as he sat in his cell and prayed for relief from the pain.

His thoughts drifted back to the minister's words. *"Redemption is a journey, not a destination. Each step brings you closer to the light, even when the path seems the darkest."*

CHAPTER 9

Savannah woke early, dawn seeping in through the window of her room. Every ounce of her body ached from doing chores she wasn't used to. The smell of strong coffee made its way under the door, and she pulled the blanket over her head, hoping to grasp a few more minutes of sleep.

She could hear her mother-in-law busy at work in the kitchen below and threw her blankets off with attitude. She dressed quickly, pulling on the plain dress. The still foreign pins were becoming easier, and, with a twinge of annoyance, she prepared for another day of chores and learning.

In the kitchen, she found Priscilla already busy preparing breakfast. "Good morning, Savannah. Did you sleep well?"

"Tell me again why we have to get up this early?"

Priscilla didn't respond but pointed to the egg basket by the back door.

Without ignoring the prompting, Savannah stepped outside, feeling the cool September air on her face. The henhouse was a small, rustic structure, and she hesitated momentarily before stepping inside. She had already had one confrontation with Rusty, the resident rooster, and she wasn't too excited to have another. The hens clucked quietly as she gently collected the eggs and placed them into the basket. Just as she was about to leave, the aggressive rooster reared his spurs and cornered her, flapping his wings and crowing loudly.

She screamed, dropping the basket of eggs. David came running from the barn. "Hold on. I'm coming!" he shouted.

David entered the coop, laughing as he shooed the rooster away. "Looks like Rusty isn't too happy with your visit this morning."

Savannah gathered the eggs that weren't broken and slipped out of the pen while David kept the rooster at bay. "Stupid bird!" she exclaimed.

"You just need to show him who's boss," he muttered as he closed the door behind him.

"It's a bird, for Pete's sake. I shouldn't be afraid of him."

"Old Rusty there likes to show his true colors occasionally, and I guess he thought he might be able to intimidate you."

"Not too many people or birds have that effect on me," Savannah said curtly.

David raised one eyebrow. "*Jah*, I've noticed that about you."

Savannah glared at him suspiciously. "Not sure if I should take that as a compliment or an insult."

"Take it how you like," he said as he walked away.

Savannah wasn't sure how she should take Neal's brother. It was like his comment was meant for a tease, but not completely.

Returning to the house, she had to admit to Priscilla she came almost empty-handed. "I had another run-in with Rusty."

"That old bird can be quite a character. The key is to never turn your back to him."

"Well, why didn't David tell me that?"

With a delicate shrug, Priscilla replied, "Could be he wanted a good laugh or two."

"It was nothing to laugh about. It nearly scared me to death."

"Come now, Savannah. It wasn't that bad. Let's put it behind us and get breakfast on the table. We have a full day of chores before the rain sets in this afternoon."

153

After breakfast, they headed to the garden. The early fall day was cool, and the garden felt peaceful with its drying plants and falling leaves. Priscilla handed her a hoe. "We'll start by pulling up the last weeds and preparing the soil for winter."

Kicking her shoes off at the garden's edge, Priscilla asked, "Ever gone barefoot on tilled soil?"

With a thoughtful expression, Savannah had to think for a minute. "I guess I can't remember the last time. So I'd have to say no."

Priscilla's smile filled her face. "You haven't experienced life until you've walked barefoot on *Gott's* earth."

Priscilla's enthusiasm showed, and Savannah couldn't help but follow suit. She took the hoe, and they worked in complete silence, the rhythmic sound of their labor soothing.

"Priscilla," Savannah began, pausing slightly, "how did you come to embrace the Amish way of life so fully?"

Without thinking, she replied, "This life is all I've ever known. It's a part of me that is as natural as breathing."

Savannah nodded, feeling respect for her commitment. "I'm starting to understand, but I can honestly say I'm not sure I could do it for long."

There was something in the way that Priscilla dug her hoe deeper after her comment that puzzled Savannah. She surely hoped her mother-in-law didn't think she could leave her old life for something as backward as an Amish lifestyle.

She barely had time to complete her thought before the older woman asked, "So where does that leave you and Neal?"

Savannah leaned on her hoe. "I guess that's up to Neal. Do you think he'll want to return to his old life?"

Priscilla wiped her brow on the back of her hand and stood straight. "Like I said, the Amish lifestyle runs deep in a person. It's difficult to leave it all behind without some big sacrifices."

Savannah stayed quiet, not wanting to upset her mother-in-law further. After a few minutes, she gathered enough thoughts to state, "I've never been very religious, and I can see faith is woven into your daily life."

Priscilla paused, stopping her garden tool in midair. "Faith is our foundation. It guides us and gives us strength. We believe everything happens according to *Gott's* will, and we find peace in that knowledge."

"Even the death of those three boys? How can that be in God's will?"

In a somber tone, Priscilla answered, "Yes, even the death of those boys. Ultimately, *Gott* is in control, and if we could see His bigger plan, we could see how something bad will eventually be part of something good."

Savannah listened intently as Priscilla returned to hoeing, still sharing her thoughts. "During difficult times, I have to believe it's *Gott's* way of turning our minds heavenward."

Priscilla made it to the end of the row, picked up a handful of weeds, and waited until Savannah had caught up to her before continuing. "Faith is a journey, not a destination. It's about trusting in His plan, even when we don't understand it. And it's never too late to start that journey."

Throughout the rest of the day, Savannah muddled over what Priscilla had shared. She couldn't help but wonder if God was in control, why would he drop her in the middle of Amish country? What lesson or good would come of stepping back into the nineteenth century? She couldn't wrap her head around His plan.

***

Harold was in the barn tending to a horse when he heard the familiar sound of buggy wheels crunching on the gravel driveway. He turned to see Bishop Weaver pull up beside the barn.

"Goot meiya, Harold," Bishop Weaver greeted as he stepped down from his buggy. The aged man's eyes were serious, and Harold sensed it wasn't a casual visit.

"Meiya, Bishop," Harold replied as he led his horse back to the corral and locked the gate behind him.

The bishop glanced around, his eyes stopping on Savannah across the barnyard, struggling with a wheelbarrow. She was dressed in Amish clothes, her awkward movements revealing her unfamiliarity with the tasks. Keeping his voice low, the bishop shared, "I heard from Neal."

Relief covered Harold's face. "You did? How is he?"

"He's... well enough. He's in a place where he's facing his mistakes and trying to make amends. But he's not ready to come home yet."

Harold's reprieve was tempered by concern. "I'll keep it to myself until he reveals himself."

The bishop's expression hardened as he watched Savannah. "There's something else. The community is in an uproar about that young woman staying with you. They're worried she might influence some of the younger girls with her worldly ways."

In a calm and severe tone, Harold replied, "I understand your concern. But she's Neal's *fraa*, and she has every right to be here and learn about our ways. I'll not turn her away, especially now."

Bishop Weaver frowned. "I know who she is, but she's still an outsider. The young ones are impressionable whether we like it or not. We need to protect our community values."

Harold met the bishop's stern glare with his own steady one. "I'll keep a close eye on her. But Neal was never baptized; he doesn't fall under the church's rule. He wasn't shunned and can still have a relationship with his family. I refuse to turn my back on either of them."

The bishop's shoulders slumped. "I understand your position. But remember that our first loyalty is to the church and its teachings. Keep her behavior in check. We can't afford to have disruptions."

As the bishop turned to leave, Harold watched Savannah fight with the wheelbarrow again. He felt a twinge of pity and admiration for her determination. He was caught between being loyal to his family and his church, and it disturbed him deeply that he might have to choose.

Harold walked over to Savannah and offered his assistance. "Here, let me help you with that."

Savannah's face, flushed from exertion, gladly stepped aside. "It's heavier than I thought."

Harold smiled gently, guiding the wheelbarrow to the compost pile. "You're giving your muscles a workout. Soon, you'll be as strong as the rest of us around here."

Harold couldn't shake the bishop's warning as they worked to empty the last of the garden weeds onto the pile. But he was determined to find a way to honor his family and faith. He hoped that in time, the community would accept Savannah, just as he was beginning to enjoy her lively spirit.

Harold straightened, brushing the dirt from his hands and taking hold of the wheelbarrow. "I'll take this from here." Savannah waved him off and headed to the house.

He must admit that her presence had brought a new energy to their home. It wasn't just her spirited nature, but her willingness to learn and adapt to all they asked of her. And even though Priscilla would never admit it, he sensed she was warming up to her as much as he was.

Harold chuckled to himself, recalling how she had struggled with the straight pins a couple of weeks ago. Despite her initial frustration, she had taken it in stride, laughing at her clumsiness, and moments like these made him see a different side of her—a side that was eager to belong.

***

After morning chores, Priscilla encouraged Savannah to walk around the farm or visit Sarah for a few hours. With Sarah being her only other connection to this new world, she wholeheartedly accepted Priscilla's offer to take a break from their regular routine.

Cutting through the field, she felt the warm morning sun on her back, the gentle rustle of falling leaves fluttering to the ground, and the sounds of nature around her. For a few minutes, she stood in awe of the splendor of her new surroundings.

When she arrived, she found Sarah hanging laundry on the line. "Savannah, I'm glad you stopped by."

"Priscilla suggested I take the morning off, and I jumped at the chance."

"I'm happy you came... but I only have a few minutes. I'm heading over to my sister-in-law's house. We're having a Sister's Day."

"Sister's Day?" Savannah asked with a bewildered smile.

"*Jah*, Emma and Samuel are hosting church this Sunday, and we're all going over to help her clean." Sarah dropped a few clothespins in the bucket at her feet. "Would you like to come?"

Savannah hesitated. "I'm not sure I'll fit in with a group of Amish women."

"Nonsense. Emma and her sisters would love to meet you. I've told them all about you. Join us, it'll be fun."

"Are you sure I wouldn't be intruding?"

"Intruding? No. You'd be bringing two more work hands. They'll love it."

Still unsure, Savannah followed Sarah back to the house.

"Let me grab the sandwiches I made for lunch, and we can go. Emma and Samuel live down the road. Walking there will only take a few minutes or so."

Emma and Samuel's charming farmhouse, nestled among tall pine trees, was set back from the road. Savannah was enveloped by the warm, welcoming atmosphere when they approached the front porch.

"Savannah, this is Emma, and these are her sisters, Rebecca and Anna."

"Welcome, Savannah!" Emma greeted her with a friendly smile. "We're glad you could join us."

They spent a better part of the day cleaning every square inch of the house, and in a weird, satisfying way, Savannah had to admit she enjoyed herself more than she'd like to admit.

The women chatted and laughed as they scrubbed and polished, making Savannah feel at ease. They were curious about her life, and she was equally intrigued by their Amish customs.

During a break, they gathered in the kitchen for a bite. Rebecca, known for her straightforward nature, turned to Savannah with a serious look. "So, what do you plan on doing if Neal doesn't come back?"

Sarah threw a disgusted. "Tsk" in Rebecca's direction.

Rebecca stiffened her shoulders. "I'm curious, is all."

Her question caught Savannah off guard. She hadn't allowed herself to think about that possibility. "I don't know," she admitted. "I haven't really thought about it."

"Would you return to Charleston?" Emma asked gently.

For the first time, Savannah realized she couldn't go back to her old life. "No, I can't. It won't feel like home anymore."

With an inviting smile, Emma asked, "Would you consider staying here? Samuel is one of the ministers at the New Order Fellowship and is much more open to letting *Englishers* attend our worship, if you're interested."

"I've not been to many church services. I wouldn't know what to do." Savannah shyly replied.

Sarah poured a fresh glass of meadow tea and took a long sip before setting it aside. She opened her hands wide, gesturing to the group. "You see this?" she began.

Savannah looked around, puzzled. "You mean, having tea and sandwiches?"

"Well, yes, that too. But more importantly, we are the church. This gathering, this fellowship, this is what church is about. We believe the church isn't just a building; it's the people, the community, a way of doing life as one unified group."

The thought of being part of a community was surprisingly appealing. "I don't know," Savannah said slowly.

"Just think about it," Sarah added. "That's why our church meets in homes. It reminds us that faith and fellowship can be found in the simplest gatherings."

Anna, who had been quietly listening, smiled. "And it's not just about us women; it's about our families, our neighbors. We are all connected, and that is what strengthens our faith."

Anna brushed crumbs from the table into her hand, saying, "It's about keeping Christ in our lives, our actions, our words, and our deeds; they all reflect our faith."

Later, as Savannah returned to the Zook farm, she reflected on all the girls had shared with her. Despite their warmth and openness, she couldn't shake a lingering unease. While there was an overwhelming sense of peace and belonging, she was afraid to become too attached to Willow Springs. Fearing it would disappoint her, much like everything else in her life had done thus far.

***

Later that afternoon, Savannah was peeling potatoes in Priscilla's kitchen. The repetitive motion allowed her to think about all the girls' words and how she really felt about staying in Willow Springs.

Even with her growing comfort, she couldn't shake the inner conflict troubling her. There were times when she missed the fast-paced, convenient lifestyle, but at the same time, she was drawn to the strong sense of community and deep-rooted values she was learning from the Zooks.

Her stay had become more about discovering herself than it was about securing a job with Mrs. Sorensen. While she pondered her dual identities, Priscilla walked in unnoticed.

"Something on your mind?" Priscilla pointed to the pile of potato peels in the sink. "Pretty soon, there won't be anything left of that potato."

Savannah dropped the peeler in the sink. "I'm feeling conflicted today. I've always been independent and sure of what I wanted out of life. But ever since I've been here and around you and Harold, I've felt a different kind of strength, a sense of fitting in I've never known."

Priscilla sat down. "Change is never easy. And who says you have to pick one over another? Why can't you take the best of both worlds and create a life that feels true to you?"

"I guess I'm afraid of losing myself."

"You're not losing yourself," Priscilla assured her. "You're growing, and growth often involves letting go of old parts to make room for new ones."

Savannah sat beside Priscilla, and with a small catch of her breath, she moaned. "I wish Neal would come home."

Priscilla patted the back of her hand. "*Jah...* me too."

CHAPTER 10

Harold and Priscilla offered to drop Savannah off at her grandmother's on their way into town. As they harnessed the horse and attached the buggy, Savannah watched with fascination. As they set off, Savannah teased, "You know I could have gotten you to the market and back in a fraction of the time if you would have let me take my car."

Harold chuckled. "We don't need the bishop seeing you dressed like that and driving a car. No, let's keep things as they are. Besides, it will be good for you to learn to go at a slower pace."

"I just don't understand the big deal with cars."

Priscilla smiled and turned to Savannah in the back of the buggy. "Cars scatter people far away from each other, but horses and buggies keep our people close together, especially our families."

"*Englisch* people are always in a hurry and busy," Harold added. "Amish people are not like that."

Savannah couldn't help but agree. Since staying with the Zooks, she felt calmer. The absence of constant distractions allowed her to focus on what truly mattered.

Harold pulled up to her grandmother's house. "We'll see you in a couple of hours."

***

Once inside, Gigi led Savannah to the kitchen, where the comforting aroma of freshly baked bread filled the air. They sat at the table, and Gigi made them coffee.

"Looks like you're settling in well with the Zook's," Gigi began, her eyes twinkling with warmth.

"They've been very patient with me."

"I'm glad to hear that." Gigi sliced the bread, spreading it with butter and honey, just as Savannah liked. "It's good you're learning their ways. This will help you understand your husband more."

Savannah's tone took on a thoughtful note. "I'd been so caught up in making a name for myself that I'd forgotten what it means to live and enjoy the simple things. The Zooks enjoy life, and I have to say it hasn't been as bad as I thought it would be."

Gigi reached across the table and squeezed Savannah's hand. "Sometimes, it takes a change of pace to see what truly matters."

"I've been thinking a lot about Neal," Savannah admitted. "About our life together and how different things could be if we embraced some of these Amish values."

Gigi nodded. "It's never too late to make changes. Sometimes, we need to slow down and listen to our heart to really hear it."

"That's funny. Harold taught me a lesson in slowing down just this morning. Seems like that's my lesson for the day." Savannah smiled. "And to think, when I first got here, I couldn't imagine staying overnight, let alone almost a month now. If my friends in Charleston could see me now."

Gigi sipped her coffee before adding, "They'd see a woman still full of spunk, but with a new sense of direction, I reckon."

They finished their tea and headed out to the front porch.

"Seen Dad lately?" Savannah asked with a skeptical tone.

Gigi smiled a warm grin that spread from ear to ear. "I think he's off with an old friend today."

"An old friend? He has friends here in Willow Springs?"

"He did grow up here... of course, he has friends. One in particular."

"Gigi? What do you know that you're not telling me?"

"Not my story to tell. But I haven't seen him smile as much as he has been the last couple of weeks, and he's stopped by almost every day."

"I'm sorry I missed that," Savannah exclaimed.

Gigi set her rocking chair in motion with her toe and tenderly added, "Your mother called yesterday. She said she'd been trying to reach you, but your phone keeps going to voicemail."

"What did she want this time?" Savanna snapped.

"I don't know, but I promised to give you her message."

They sat for a few minutes before Gigi got the nerve to add her thoughts about the situation with her mother. "Perhaps it would help if you tried to reach out to her. I'm certain she'd love to talk to you." Gigi paused, deep in thought of her own past, and sighed. "You know, I didn't always do the right thing by your dad. I made mistakes—big ones. But I learned I couldn't blame his behavior on my mistakes forever. It took me a long time to figure out that I couldn't write his testimony, just like you can't write your mother's."

Savannah looked over at her. "What do you mean?"

"She's a grown woman and subject to making her own mistakes. It's not your place to indefinitely bind her or your father to past slip-ups. It's not healthy for you or her. If you truly searched your heart, you'd see that you want reconciliation as much as she does."

Savannah groaned. "Gigi, you know how Mom gets. We can barely speak a civil word to one another before one of us spouts off something ugly, and all war breaks out."

Gigi sighed and paused long before adding, "But you're different now. Perhaps the changes you're making in your life will help curb some of that built-up frustration you feel toward her." Gigi rocked her chair a few times before finishing. "Savannah, my dear, she's still your mother, and you need to learn to accept your differences as part of what makes you each unique."

"And when was the last time she acted like my mother?"

"Now, Savannah… she loves you enough to call and check on you. That has to count for something."

Savannah laid her head back on the rocking chair and sighed. "I know, Gigi, but I have difficulty getting over everything we've gone through."

Gigi softened her voice, hoping to appeal to Savannah's heart. "Remember, my dear, forgiveness is a gift we've been freely given, and it's a gift we are called to offer others. Holding onto that hurt will only keep you bound to bitterness. Forgiveness can heal wounds that otherwise would go untreated. You have to start somewhere, and perhaps returning her call is a good place to start."

"I'll think about it, Gigi. I really will."

Gigi tenderly laid a hand on Savannah's arm. "I promise you, once you offer forgiveness, you'll find peace in letting go of the bitterness attached to your heart. Maybe it's time to try and offer that to her, even if it's just a small step."

Gigi returned to the house, leaving Savannah alone on the porch. She pulled her sweater close to ward off the chilly air as the sun dipped behind a cloud. She sat there, her thoughts tangled in the crisp breeze, her heart heavy with her grandmother's words.

The idea of forgiveness and letting go of the past lingered in her mind. Closing her eyes, she tried to remember happier times with her mom—moments when the two were laughing and enjoying each other's company.

A memory floated to the surface: a sunny, warm day at the lake, her mother's laughter blending with the sound of the water lapping against the shore. They collected pretty stones and shared ice cream cones. She could still feel the warmth of her mother's hand in hers; love had been so easy then.

Another memory surfaced, this one of a rainy afternoon. They had stayed indoors, creating art projects and baking cookies. Her mother taught her how to measure flour and crack eggs, her patience endless and her smile unwavering. She could still remember the smell of chocolate in the air as she watched her mother warmly greet her father as he arrived home.

Tears rose in her eyes as she relived those special moments. The memories were bittersweet, a reminder of what had been lost but also a testament to the love that they once shared.

Savannah knew she wasn't yet strong enough to offer forgiveness, but for the first time, she felt like someday she might be. She took a long breath, the cold air filling her lungs, and closed her eyes. She wasn't used to praying but whispered a quiet plea for guidance.

"God, I don't know if you're listening or if I even know how to do this right," she began, her voice trembling. *"But if you can hear me, please help me find the strength to forgive. Help me see the path forward and mend the broken pieces of my heart."*

The wind rustled the last few falling leaves, and Savannah felt a strange calm. It wasn't an answer, but it was a start. She opened her eyes, wiped away the tears, and sat a little longer, letting the stillness of the day wrap around her.

***

Savannah's mornings at the Zook farm had settled into a comforting routine. But today was different. Priscilla had mentioned a community barn-raising, and Savannah was eager to participate. This would be her first big community event, and she hoped it would help her integrate further into the Amish way of life.

She dressed quickly, pinning her apron and securing her hair under her *kapp*, now a familiar routine. The day promised hard work, but she was ready.

174

When they arrived at the barn-raising site, Savannah was struck by the sheer number of people. Men, women, and older children moved in a well-choreographed dance of cooperation. She was immediately put to work, joining a group of women preparing food for the workers.

The women welcomed her, but she could feel their curiosity. Savannah listened to their conversations as they kneaded dough and chopped vegetables, gradually joining in. She shared stories from her life in Charleston, earning her a mix of gasps and laughter.

Savannah worked alongside her friend Sarah, who was kind and patient, explaining the jobs as they went along.

"I'm really enjoying this," Savannah whispered, wiping sweat from her brow. "It's a different kind of work, but it feels good."

When Sarah stepped away to retrieve something from the porch, a young dark-haired woman stepped beside Savannah.

"You're *Englisch*, right?" her tone was cold.

"Yes," Savannah replied, trying to keep her tone level.

"And you think you can just walk in here and fit in? It's not that simple."

Savannah took a deep breath. "I know it's not, and I don't expect it to be easy. But I'm here to learn and help however I can."

The girl's eyes narrowed. "We'll see about that."

The words stung, but Savannah refused to be discouraged. She worked harder, determined to prove herself. Later, as Savannah served the workers food, the same woman confronted her again.

"You don't belong here," she said harshly. "You'll never understand our ways. You should go back to where you came from."

Savannah's temper flared. "I'm trying my best to learn and fit in. What gives you the right to judge me?"

The girl was clearly agitated. Clutching her arms across her chest, she muttered, "You're an outsider. You can't just come here and expect us to accept you."

Savannah's voice rose. "I'm not here to disrupt anything. I'm here to learn, help, and join this community."

Their exchange drew the attention of others, and Sarah overheard the conversation, then Sarah quickly intervened. "Let's take a walk," Sarah said gently.

Once they were away from the hustle and bustle, Sarah began, "I heard what Rosalie said to you. It wasn't kind, but we must remember our ways. Confrontation isn't our way. We must show patience and kindness, even when others don't."

Savannah sighed in frustration. "I just want to fit in."

Sarah smiled gently. "I know you do. And you will. But it takes time. The Amish way of life is about more than just actions; it's about the heart. Let your actions speak for you. Show them your dedication through your work and your kindness. That's how you'll win them over."

"I'll try to remember that even when my insides are screaming anything but."

Later, Sarah found Savannah sitting quietly on the porch, clearly still affected by her encounter with Rosalie.

"Hey, are you okay?" Sarah asked, sitting down beside her.

Savannah shrugged. "I don't know. Rosalie really got to me. Some people don't want to accept me, no matter how hard I try. I could feel the coldness in the room after that girl confronted me."

Sarah sighed. "I should have told you earlier. Rosalie stepped out with Neal a few times before the accident and before he ran away. I'm certain she has a lot of unresolved feelings simmering just beneath the surface."

Savannah's eyes widened in surprise at Sarah's comment.

Sarah nodded. "That's why she was so harsh. It's not just because you're *Englisch*; it's because of her history with Neal."

Savannah felt a pang of guilt and sympathy. "That makes sense. I wish she could see I'm not here to cause trouble."

"She'll come around in time," Sarah assured her. "Meanwhile, just keep being you."

Savannah smiled, feeling a bit lighter. "She does know Neal and I are married, right?"

"I'm sure she does, but that doesn't help heal her emotions. I'm sure seeing you is just a harsh reminder of the hope she needs to let go of."

"I'm sorry she's hurting... but aren't we all these days?"

***

Savannah adjusted the plain dress she had become accustomed to over the past thirty days. The transition from her fancy clothes to the unadorned Amish dress had been challenging but also brought a surprising sense of comfort. As she walked to the Apple Blossom Inn, nerves churned in her stomach. She could see the inn in the distance; its charming façade made her excited and anxious.

Suddenly, a wave of nausea hit her. She stepped off the path and leaned against a tree, trying to steady her breathing. She felt her stomach churn again, and she was sick in the weeds before she could stop it. Wiping her mouth with the back of her hand, she took a few deep breaths, trying to compose herself. "Must be nerves," she muttered, shaking her head.

After a few minutes, she straightened and continued her walk to the inn, determined not to let her sour stomach get in the way of her interview. The sickening sweet smell of apple pie hit her as she pushed open the oak door, forcing her to swallow hard before greeting Mrs. Sorensen.

Mrs. Sorensen looked stern; her graying hair pulled back into a bun so tight it seemed to pull her expression taut. She eyed Savannah from head to toe. "Savannah."

"Mrs. Sorensen," Savannah replied, trying to keep her queasiness under control.

"I see you've embraced plain dress."

"Yes, ma'am," Savannah nodded. "I've spent the last month living with the Zook family, learning as much as possible from them."

"And what have you learned?" Mrs. Sorensen asked, her expression unreadable.

Savannah's tongue flicked out and wetted her lips before she answered. "I've learned the importance of community, hard work, and humility. Their way of life has taught me to slow down and appreciate the simple things. It's also given me a new perspective on forgiveness and patience."

Mrs. Sorensen's tone was casual as she replied, "I must say, you do seem different from the last time we met. You seem calmer and less high-spirited."

The older woman looked her over again, adding, "This job won't be easy. You'll have to navigate the expectations of our English customers while respecting Amish values and beliefs. How do you plan to handle that?"

Savannah thought with an inward smile. "I'll ensure our guests understand the importance of respect and simplicity when interacting with the Amish community."

Mrs. Sorensen studied her for a moment, then nodded. "You can start tomorrow morning."

Savannah's heart skipped a beat. "Thank you."

"Your first task will be to organize the Apple Butter Festival. I have volunteered to use our grounds for the event. You have a month to consolidate all the vendors and plan the day's events. It's a significant event for the inn, and it must go off without a hitch."

Walking back to the Zooks', Savannah's mind raced with ideas and plans for the festival. Her new responsibilities settled on her shoulders, and she only had a month to pull it off.

The crisp air felt good on her skin, and she couldn't help but smile, thinking how far she'd come and how much further she had to go. As she neared home, Priscilla was waiting on the porch, a knowing smile on her face.

"So? How did it go?"

"I start tomorrow. My first job is to organize the Apple Butter Festival."

Savannah followed Priscilla back into the kitchen and sat at the table. Priscilla returned to peeling apples, her hands moving with the practiced ease of someone who had done it countless times. Savannah was excited to discuss the upcoming event. "How do you make apple butter? Mrs. Sorensen said she wants everything to be authentic, and I want to make sure I get it right," Savannah asked as she picked up a pen and paper from the center of the table.

Priscilla set down her paring knife and wiped her hands on her apron. "Oh, it's quite a process and something special. First, we spend weeks preparing the apples for snitzing. And hours and hours drying the apples to the perfect texture before storing them in covered buckets.

Then, on the morning of the actual butter-making day, we make bread dough for a special treat with the warm apple butter—fresh bread. The men start a fire under large copper kettles, and we add the snitzed apples, cider, and sugar. We all take turns pushing large wooden stirrers back and forth to keep the apple butter from burning."

Priscilla smiled as the memories flooded her mind. "It was the highlight of the fall season when I was a child. My *mamm* would give us pennies to throw in the pot that would be pushed back and forth to keep it from scorching. Those pennies would become prize possessions after the butter had been ladled out."

Priscilla pulled a chair out and sat beside her. "There are always lots of activities for the children at the festival, like bobbing for apples and sack races. The adults enjoy the quilt auction and homemade crafts, and the pie-eating contest is always a big hit."

Savannah's eyes widened in surprised pleasure. "That sounds perfect!" Savannah smiled, feeling more confident about her role. "I just want to do it justice. I've already got a few ideas, but I want to ensure they honor the community."

Priscilla gave her a nervous nod. "Remember, Savannah, simple... nothing over the top."

Savannah felt a warm rush of gratitude at Priscilla's concern. "Thank you... I'll keep that in mind."

CHAPTER 11

Neal stood on the porch, his heart pounding. He took a deep breath and slowly opened the door. The familiar creak of the old hinges filled the air, and he stepped inside. The scent of fresh bread and roasted meat greeted him, returning his childhood memories.

Moving toward the kitchen, he heard voices. He stopped, peering through the doorway. In the kitchen was Savannah, standing beside his mother, wearing a plain dress, her hair pulled and tucked neatly under a white *kapp*. His mother at the sink and his father at the table. She moved with such a calm grace, something he'd never seen before in his wife. The sight took his breath away. He stood frozen, unable to comprehend what he was witnessing. Savannah, the woman who had always let everyone know she was in the room, was quiet and working peacefully beside his mother, her movements graceful. He blinked, wondering if he was dreaming or perhaps in the wrong house.

His mother glanced up and saw him standing in the doorway. A warm, welcoming smile spread across her face. "Neal, you're home," she said tenderly.

Savannah turned, her eyes meeting his. Instead of the anger and hurt he expected, he saw quiet acceptance. His heart ached with everything he'd put her through. "Savannah," he said in barely a whisper.

His mother wiped her hands on her apron, laid her hand on her husband's shoulder, and said, "We'll leave the two of you alone."

"Not yet. I have so much to explain first." For the next thirty minutes, Neal told his parents and Savannah about his false identity, his charges in Charleston, and his decision to face the circumstances on his own. He went into great detail about how he wanted to make amends and prayed they would accept his heartfelt apology.

After Neal's parents left Savannah and him alone, Neal stepped closer, his eyes never leaving Savannah's face. "You... you look so different. What's with the Amish clothes?"

Savannah offered him a small smile while she tucked a loose hair back under her *kapp*. "Much has changed since you've been gone. I've been discovering what it's like to be Amish and getting to know your parents."

He took a step closer, his heart racing. She took a step back when he tried to reach out to her. "I'm not going to lie, Neal," she began, "I'm angry and hurt that you chose to run away when you had problems we should have faced together."

Neal's eyes filled with tenderness. "I don't deserve you; I never did."

Savannah waved her hands and asked, "Why didn't you tell me about all this?"

He reached out, taking her hands in his. "It was wrong to hide all this from you, but there were so many things about this place that reminded me of the pain I caused. I thought if I locked it all away, reinvented who I was, I could rid myself of the shame."

She stepped closer and whispered, "I know about the boys."

The tender way in which she laid a hand on his cheek made him utter a short, anguished moan. "Oh… Savannah, I've done so many things wrong; will you ever forgive me?"

"I'm sure I will in time. But for now, we need to start over. I don't want to return to how we were, especially after spending the last month with your parents. It's the best thing that could have happened to me. Your parents have taught me so much about your way of life that has made me rethink some of my own life choices... even some of my choices when it comes to you."

"What does that mean for us?" he asked.

"I'm not really sure, but now that you're home, we can discuss it... that is, if you're here to stay."

Neal pulled her into his arms, holding her close. The warmth of her body against his brought a sense of home he hadn't felt in a long time. "Thank you for waiting for me."

She rested her head against his chest. "I'm not going to say it was easy, but I know it was in the Lord's plan for me to come to Willow Springs." They stood still for a few minutes, wrapped in each other's embrace, before Neal asked, "Just how did you find me?"

"I didn't... God did."

He hugged her tighter and chuckled. "Who are you, and what did you do with my wife?"

"Your *fraa* is the same person she's always been... just a little wiser and a whole lot more sure of what she wants out of life."

Neal's heart was about to burst when the small *Deitsh* word slipped from her lips. He had never been more in love or thought she looked prettier than she did right at the moment. He closed his eyes and silently thanked *Gott* for bringing him home.

***

Neal sat in the old wooden chair, the familiar creak of its legs against the old pine floor echoing through the quiet room. His father sat across from him, his face carved in worry. Bishop Weaver sat beside his father, both their eyes fixed on his.

"Neal," the bishop began, his voice calm yet firm, "we're here to discuss your plans now that you've returned. Are you planning on staying?"

"I want to stay, but I've not spoken to Savannah about it yet. I wanted to take it slow... I must regain her trust, which won't be easy." Neal shifted in his chair and continued, "I know that for us to move forward, I need to get my priorities in the right order. Beginning with putting *Gott* first in my life."

Harold nodded. "That's a good place to start, son."

The bishop leaned back, his eyes narrowing thoughtfully. "You've complicated things by marrying outside the fold, and I'm not certain your wife could convert to our ways."

Neal hesitated, choosing his words carefully. "I agree. Savannah wouldn't do well in the Old Order Church, and I'd never ask her to give up her life for mine."

Harold quickly added, "She's made tremendous strides in understanding our way of life, but it's a lot to ask of her to fully immerse herself into the Old Order."

"I won't ask her to do that. We need a balance of both worlds, and at this point, I don't know what that looks like."

Bishop Weaver tapped his thumbs on the arm of his chair, slowly nodding, contemplating Neal's statement. "It sounds like you've given this a lot of thought. But you understand it won't be easy. Eventually, you'll need to commit to one way or another."

"I understand that," Neal replied. "I'm willing to do whatever it takes to make things right in this community and with Savannah."

The bishop looked serious. "In the meantime, I suggest you and Savannah live separately. This period of separation will allow both of you to work on yourselves and your relationship with *Gott*."

Neal nodded without saying a word, already playing the conversation with Savannah over in his head.

The bishop smiled as he slid to the edge of his chair. "Please remember, it's not just about proving yourself; it's about finding your way back to the Lord."

Before he stood to leave, Neal cleared his throat, a look of determination in his eyes. "There's something else... I've written to each family of the three boys. I've asked to meet with them. I need to do it to make amends to move forward."

The bishop agreed. "Reconciliation is the cornerstone of our faith, and seeking forgiveness is part of your journey."

"Also, I think I'd like to meet with Bishop Schrock. I hear the New Order Fellowship church is more welcoming to *Englishers*. Savannah might fit in better there."

Harold looked at his son with understanding eyes. "I think that's a better fit for you both."

***

Later that afternoon, Savannah and Neal walked down the winding dirt path leading to the back of the Zook property. The air was filled with the scent of fallen leaves and the distant sound of birds chirping. Savannah felt lighter as she shared her excitement about her new job at the Apple Blossom Inn.

"The Apple Butter Festival is going to be amazing. It's a big responsibility, but I'm ready for it."

"I'm so happy you've found a place for yourself here, and it sounds like an incredible opportunity."

Savannah looped her arm in Neal's. "I can honestly say when I first showed up at Gigi's, I didn't think I'd make it through the night, but I've learned to see the beauty of the simpler way of life. Who would have thought?"

"Not me... for sure!"

They walked in a comfortable silence for a few moments, the serenity of the countryside enveloping them. But as they approached the edge of the field, Neal's demeanor shifted. He seemed more thoughtful; his eyes clouded with something unspoken.

"Savannah," he started, stopping and turning to face her, "there's something we need to talk about."

The tone of his voice sent a fresh ripple of unease through her. "What is it?"

His melancholy seemed to deepen. "I want us to build a strong foundation for our marriage. One that's not built on lies and secrecy."

"I want that too," she whispered.

He took her hands in his. "There are things I need to make right with God and within myself before I can fully give myself to you again."

Savannah's heart sank. "What does that mean?"

"I'm saying that I think it's best if you move back to your grandmother's house for a while. I'll stay here with my parents. The time apart will give us the space we need to heal and grow. I know it's not what you need to hear, but I truly believe it's what we must do."

Savannah felt a surge of old, ugly bitterness creeping into her heart, and she pulled her hand from his. "So you want me to just pack up and leave? After everything we've been through, you're asking me to go?"

Neal reached out, his hand brushing her arm, and she jerked away. "Please understand. This isn't about pushing you away. It's about doing things right." He paused, gauging his words before continuing. "I'm not even sure we are legally married, and I need to figure out how to clean up the mess I've made."

Savannah's eyes filled with tears of frustration. "How can you expect me to trust you when you ask me to leave? It feels like you're abandoning me all over again."

"I'm not abandoning you. I'm trying to do what's best for us. Please, give me this time. Trust that this is part of our journey, and I must travel alone for a little while."

Savannah pulled away, wrapping her arms around herself to shield her heart. "I don't understand why we can't stay together and work through this."

"I wish it were that simple. But this is what I feel in my heart. It's what I believe God wants us to do."

"What about me?" Savannah cried. "Have you thought about what I might want or need? It seems we're returning to where we were two months ago. You live in your private world, and I'm grasping to understand what's happening inside your head."

Neal moved closer, his voice tender. "I'm asking you to trust me one more time. To trust in God's plan for us."

The silence between them stretched, filled with unspoken emotions. Savannah turned away, wiping a tear from her cheek.

"I don't like this, but I'll give you your time. However, know it'll be hard for me... really hard."

On their way back to the farmhouse, Savannah couldn't shake the feeling of uncertainty. The peace she had gained over the past thirty days seemed to slip away, replaced with a lingering doubt.

Neal brushed her hand and locked his finger around one of her fingers. "Thank you. I promise I'll do everything to make this up to you."

***

The following day, they met with Bishop Schrock, the bishop of the New Order Fellowship Church. They sat side by side at the bishop's kitchen table. The middle-aged man sat across from them, listening intently as Neal and Savannah recounted their story.

"I understand your situation," Bishop Schrock said, his voice reassuring. "It's clear that you want to make things right, and that's a commendable start."

Savannah glanced at Neal, her heart heavy with uncertainty. "What do you suggest we do to rebuild our marriage?"

The bishop leaned forward, resting his hands on the table. "First, you must understand that healing takes time and patience. I suggest you take a few months to be certain Willow Springs is where you want to live and integrate into the community and possibly the church. This will allow you both to grow individually in your faith and to see if this life truly resonates with you." He waited and looked at Savannah. "This lifestyle is so different from what you know, so a decision can't be made lightly."

Neal nodded, his face serious. "I agree."

"I know that, but how do we proceed with our relationship in the meantime?" Savannah inquired.

The bishop took a breath and sat back in his chair, looking at them both intently. "I suggest you act as if you're first getting to know one another. Perhaps you start by seeing each other only on Sundays. This will give you time to reflect, pray, and seek guidance from the Lord. It will also help you build a solid foundation of faith for your marriage once you come back together."

Savannah slumped in her chair, dreading being away from Neal most of the week. "Only Sundays?" she whispered, her voice trembling with emotion.

The bishop nodded. "I know it sounds difficult, but this period of separation can be a great time of personal growth. Courtship is meant to keep our eyes focused on building a spiritual connection first. I understand you're already married, but given the circumstances, it would be wise to start anew. Build your relationship on a foundation of faith first, then work on your future."

Savannah felt slow, hot tears wetting her throat as she looked at Neal. She couldn't believe what they asked her to do, but she would agree if it meant saving her marriage and helping Neal heal. Silently, she nodded in agreement.

The bishop rose from his chair, signaling the end of their meeting. "Take this time to reflect. Attend worship services, participate in community activities, and seek guidance from the Lord. If you commit to this process, I believe you'll find the strength and clarity you need to rebuild your marriage."

Returning to the Zook farm, Savannah sat silently in the buggy, allowing the bishop's words to settle. The gentle clip-clop of the horse's hooves was a comforting rhythm, but it did little to soothe her raging emotions.

Neal's mother met them on the porch.

Savannah sighed. "He suggested we take a few months to become part of the community and only see each other on Sundays."

Neal squeezed Savannah's hand one last time before letting go. "It will go fast and give me plenty of time to prove I can be trusted again."

With a heavy heart, Savannah went inside to gather the rest of her belongings and change out of her plain clothes. She climbed the stairs slowly, each step feeling heavier than the last. Once inside the bedroom, she closed the door, leaned against it, and took a deep breath.

She moved to the dresser and pulled out her old clothes. She felt regretful as she slipped off the plain dress and apron. The Amish clothes had become a part of her. Now, falling back into her tight jeans and fitted blouse, she felt lost. The clothes clung to her body in a way that felt both familiar and alien.

Uncoiling her hair from the tight bun, she let it fall around her shoulders; the relief was immediate, but a wave of nausea came with it. She took a deep breath, settled her stomach, and ran her fingers through her hair, feeling the freedom and the loss of the peace she had gained simultaneously.

Neal knocked softly on the door and pushed it open. His eyes changed when he saw her dressed in different clothes. There was a flicker of something—perhaps disappointment? "You look so much different in those," he said timidly.

Savannah forced a smile. "Different good or different bad?"

Neal hesitated. "Just different. I guess I got used to seeing you in plain dress. It suited you."

Savannah felt a lump in her throat. "I think I'll miss it. But I need to find a balance between your world and mine."

Neal nodded, though she could see the struggle in his eyes. "I understand. It's just… you looked so at home in them. But we'll find a way to make it work for both of us."

She reached out, took his hand, and then dropped it just as fast as she remembered the bishop's warning about no touching during courtship. "I hope so."

They stood there momentarily, holding each other's gaze, trying to draw strength from each other. Finally, Savannah looked away. "I should go. Gigi is expecting me."

Neal walked her to her car. "Remember, Sundays. We'll see each other then."

She tried to muster up some enthusiasm. "Sundays."

Climbing into her car, she sucked in a breath, trying to will the tears away. Pulling away, she looked in the rearview mirror to see Neal standing in the same spot she'd left him. His expression matched the condition of her heart, reminding her that their journey was far from over... no, it had just begun.

CHAPTER 12

Savannah stood in the Apple Blossom Inn's entryway, straightening the fall flowers she had set out that morning. The dark colors of the leaves matched her unsettled mood. She had been working at the inn for a week now, and adjusting to Mrs. Sorensen's ways was challenging, to say the least.

Mrs. Sorensen entered the room, her sharp eyes scanning every detail. Savannah tensed, knowing the older woman would have something to say. She had learned to keep her thoughts to herself and take criticism gracefully, but it wasn't always easy.

"These flowers," Mrs. Sorensen began, her voice tight, "need to be fresher. We can't have wilted arrangements in the main hall."

Savannah nodded, biting her tongue. "I'll replace them right away."

"And the sign for the Apple Butter Festival out front," Mrs. Sorensen continued, her tone unwavering, "it's too modern. We want to portray a sense of old-fashioned fun. We need something simpler, more in line with the country landscape." The older woman gave her a stern look. "From now on, I want to see all marketing material before it goes to print."

Savannah felt a surge of frustration but bit her lip. "Yes, ma'am. I'll get it redesigned right away."

Mrs. Sorensen's gaze remained critical. "You're used to a different world... more trendy and flashy. But to succeed here, you'll have to understand our clientele. They value simplicity and authenticity and seek a true Amish experience when visiting Willow Springs."

Savannah felt her heart race as she tried to control her gut reaction to buck Mrs. Sorensen's reprimand. "I'll try to remember that."

Mrs. Sorensen studied her momentarily, then added briskly, "Good. Now, let's go over the plans for the festival. We need to ensure everything is perfect."

They moved to the office, and Savannah spread her plans on the desk. Mrs. Sorensen leaned over, scrutinizing each detail.

"For the live apple butter demonstration," Savannah began, "I've arranged for a few local Amish women to come and make it on-site throughout the day. They will be cooking it in large copper pots over an open fire. The smell will add a sense of ambience to the event. I've even secured a group of men to keep the fires going."

Mrs. Sorensen frowned slightly. "And who will be preparing all those apples beforehand?"

Savannah noted, "I have that already handled, and I won't need to distract the kitchen staff from their duties. I've asked a few of my Amish friends for help."

"And the activities for the children?" Mrs. Sorensen pressed.

"We'll have a petting zoo, pony rides, and traditional games. Everything is designed to be family-friendly."

Mrs. Sorensen's eyebrow arched. "I think it would be better to focus on activities that teach Amish values, like simple crafts or storytelling sessions about Amish history and culture."

Savannah took a deep breath. "That's a great idea. I'll adjust the schedule to include those activities."

"And what about the vendors? We need to make sure they fit our standards as well," Mrs. Sorensen said, her tone still sharp.

"I've personally contacted each vendor. They're all local and have agreed to adhere to the guidelines we've set for the festival," Savannah replied, feeling a bit defensive.

Mrs. Sorensen's eyes remained critical. "Ensure they understand the importance of modesty and simplicity in their presentations. No flashy signs or modern gimmicks."

Savannah sucked in a breath, determined not to let her frustration show in her responses. "I'm confident I've thought of everything and won't disappoint you. I'm committed to making this festival a success."

Mrs. Sorensen finally offered a faint smile. "I'm sure you have, but Willow Springs isn't Charleston, and I just want to make sure you understand the cultural differences you're dealing with."

Savannah left the office, feeling relieved she could keep calm and collected through Mrs. Sorensen's criticism. The challenges were daunting, but she was determined to prove herself. There was no mistaking that; adjusting to Mrs. Sorensen's exacting standards was tough. It was difficult, but each step brought her closer to the person she wanted to become. She was learning, growing, and slowly finding her place in this new world.

***

Neal stood outside the sprawling farmhouse, his thoughts mixed with the red and gold maple leaves caught in the breeze, creating a serene backdrop that did little to calm his nerves. Today, he would face the first family of the three boys who had died because of his carelessness. He'd written letters to each family; now it was time to seek their forgiveness in person.

Taking a deep breath, he knocked on the door. Moments later, it opened to reveal Mrs. King, her eyes widening in surprise.

"Neal Zook?" she said, her voice quavering with recognition.

"Mrs. King, may I come in?" he asked, his voice trembling.

She nodded slowly and stepped aside, allowing him to enter. The house's interior was warm and inviting, filled with the scent of freshly brewed coffee. Neal followed her into the living room, where Mr. King was reading a newspaper. He looked up, his expression hardening as he saw Neal.

"Mr. King," Neal began, "I've come to ask for your forgiveness."

Mr. King's eyes bored into him, but he said nothing. Mrs. King gestured for Neal to sit, and he sat on the edge of the couch, his hands clasped tightly in his lap.

"I know that my actions caused unimaginable pain," Neal said, struggling to keep his voice steady. "I'm truly sorry for what happened."

Mr. King finally spoke, his voice low and measured. "We've had many years to come to terms with our loss, Neal. The pain you've carried with guilt is far worse than ours."

Neal looked up, confusion and hope mingling in his eyes. "I don't understand."

Mrs. King took a long breath before softly adding, "When you left, we were angry and hurt. But over time, we realized that holding onto that anger wouldn't bring our son back. We had to find a way to move forward for our own sake."

Mr. King nodded. "We forgive you, Neal. It wasn't an easy journey, but our way teaches us that forgiveness frees us from the burden of anger. And now, it's time for you to be free from guilt."

Tears welled up in Neal's eyes, and he felt a crushing weight lifted from his shoulders. "Thank you," he whispered, his voice choked with emotion. "Thank you for your forgiveness."

Mrs. King smiled softly. "We pray you can focus on your own healing now that you're back. Seeking forgiveness is the first step, and we hope it brings you the peace you've been searching for."

Neal stayed longer, talking with the Kings about their son, sharing memories, and finding solace in their words. As he left the farmhouse, he felt blessed that their kind words had given him the strength to continue his journey of redemption.

***

Savannah sat on the edge of her bed, her hands trembling as she stared at the positive pregnancy test. She'd suspected as much for a few days, but seeing the confirmation before her made her feel elated and terrified. The timing couldn't be worse. She didn't know how to handle the inevitable. After a few moments of gathering her thoughts, she decided to confide in the one person she trusted the most, Gigi.

Savannah strolled down the hall to Gigi's room, the heaviness of her news pressing down on her shoulders. She knocked softly on the door and entered when she heard Gigi's gentle voice.

"Savannah, dear, what's troubling you?" Gigi asked, her eyes full of concern. Savannah sat down on the edge of the bed, her eyes welling up with tears as she held out the pregnancy test strip.

Gigi couldn't hide her excitement and only calmed after sensing Savannah's turmoil. She reached out to take Savannah's hands in hers. "Oh, Savannah. This is happy news, *no?*"

"I don't know," Savannah admitted, her voice shaking. "I'm happy, but I'm also scared. The timing couldn't be worse. I don't even know where things stand with Neal, and now this…"

Gigi squeezed Savannah's hands reassuringly. "God's timing is always perfect, even when it doesn't seem that way to us. This baby is a blessing, and you must trust that everything will work out."

Savannah laid both hands across her tummy and sighed. "But, Gigi, I never wanted children. I'm not sure I'm the motherly type, and I certainly don't want a repeat of my childhood. What if I can't handle it? What if I make mistakes?"

Gigi looked at her with a calm, steady gaze. "You can create a different family if that bothers you."

Savannah shook her head, frustrated. "But what if Neal and I don't work out? What if he can't forgive himself? I'm not sure if our marriage can survive everything, and I don't want a baby to be the reason we stay together."

Gigi smiled gently. "Savannah, you know that the Amish marry for life, don't you? Divorce isn't an option for Neal. If he's committed to making things right, then there's no way that it won't work out in the end."

Savannah wiped a tear from her cheek. Worry lines etched into her features. "But Gigi, things are different with us. We come from different worlds, and so many obstacles exist."

Gigi squeezed Savannah's hand. "Every marriage has its challenges, dear. But love, patience, and faith can overcome anything. You and Neal have been given the precious gift of a child. Use it to come together, find common ground, and build a future with both backgrounds."

Savannah felt a flicker of hope in her heart despite the lingering doubts. "I don't know how to be a mother. What if I fail?"

Gigi's eyes softened. "You're stronger than you think. You've already shown courage by coming here and trying to understand Neal's world. And now you have a new reason to be strong—for your child."

Savannah nodded, taking a deep breath. "I hope I can be as strong as you say I am."

***

Neal stood outside the Ed Miller Harness Shop, sweat forming across his brow. He knew this visit would be the hardest. The memory of Joe Miller's death was the one that hit him the hardest. The young boy looked up to him, and he bore his death the hardest. Standing outside the rustic shop, memories of his time with Ed and his sons hurt him deeply, and he doubted Ed Miller could ever truly forgive him.

The shop was bustling with activity, the rhythmic sound of tools and the scent of leather filling the air. Neal took a deep breath and stepped inside, his eyes scanning the room for Ed. He spotted him at the back, meticulously working on a harness. He approached cautiously.

"Ed," he began, his voice trembling slightly. "I came to talk to you about Joe."

Ed looked up, his expression hardening as he recognized him. He wiped his hands on a rag, his movements slow and deliberate. "What do you want?" he asked, his tone clipped.

Neal swallowed hard. "I wanted to ask for your forgiveness. I know what happened was a terrible accident, and I've carried the guilt with me every day."

Ed's eyes narrowed, and he let out a harsh laugh. "Forgiveness, huh? Our faith teaches us to forgive, so I suppose I have to say I forgive you. But don't think for a moment that it changes anything. Joe's gone, and nothing you say or do will bring him back."

Neal's shoulders sagged under Ed's words. "I understand that. I don't expect to be absolved of my guilt. I just wanted to express my regret and ask for a chance to make amends."

Ed's gaze turned cold. "Making amends won't bring back my boy. Do you think you can waltz back into this community and be forgiven? My son's life was cut short because of a silly prank. And now, Jacob's struggling to fill Joe's shoes. It's a daily reminder of what we've lost."

Neal felt a lump in his throat as he looked into Ed's eyes. The pain and resentment were real. "I know I can't change the past. But I want to be part of this community again. I want to help in any way I can."

Ed shook his head, his expression one of barely concealed anger. "Help? You've done enough damage, Neal. I'll say I forgive you because that's what the church demands, but don't expect me to welcome you back with open arms."

Neal felt the sting of Ed's words deeply. He had hoped for some semblance of reconciliation, but it was clear that the wounds were still too raw. "I'm truly sorry, Ed," he said quietly. "If there's anything I can do..."

Ed cut him off with a sharp gesture. "You've done enough. Just stay out of my way."

Feeling defeated, Neal nodded and turned to leave. As he walked out of the shop, the community's path to forgiveness and acceptance seemed more daunting than ever as he spotted Joe's younger *bruder* standing in the shadow. He felt a flicker of doubt, wondering if he could ever truly make amends for his past mistakes. The look on the young man's face bore a hole in Neal's heart and gave him reason to pause. It took him a moment to collect himself. The harsh reality of Ed's unforgiving stance went against the teachings of their faith. He knew he had to keep trying, even if it meant facing more rejection and hostility.

CHAPTER 13

Neal stood by the entrance of Bishop Shetler's home, nervously scanning the crowd for any sign of Savannah. He had invited her to church, hoping it would be a step toward rebuilding their life together. As he waited, he heard a familiar voice call his name.

"Neal! It's so good to see you back," Rosalie said sweetly, her voice flirtatious. She approached him with a bright smile, her eyes sparkling with interest.

"Hello, Rosalie," Neal replied, trying to keep his tone polite but distant.

"I heard you'd returned to Willow Springs. It's about time," she said, stepping closer to him. "We've all missed you."

Neal forced a smile, his eyes constantly darting past her, looking for any sign of Savannah. "Thank you. It's good to be back."

Rosalie whispered and leaned in a bit too close for Neal's liking. "If you had stayed, it would have been me you'd be watching for."

Neal stiffened at her words. "Rosalie, I appreciate your welcome, but your behavior is inappropriate."

Her expression shifted from sweet to offended. "Inappropriate? Neal, we grew up together. We were meant to be. At one time, I let you take me home... don't you remember?"

"Things change, Rosalie," Neal said firmly. "I'm married, so this conversation is unacceptable."

Rosalie's eyes narrowed. "If you truly loved her, you wouldn't have lied to her all these years about your past."

Neal felt his temper rise, but he kept his composure. "I made mistakes, and I'm trying to make things right."

Rosalie's face flushed with anger. "You're still making mistakes. She'll never fit in here."

"That's for us to figure out," Neal said, ending the conversation abruptly as he spotted Savannah across the yard. "Excuse me."

***

Savannah woke up early, the morning sun streaming through her window. The day felt heavy with significance. Neal had sent her a note, asking her to attend the New Order Fellowship service with him. It was a big step, and Savannah's nerves were frayed at the thought.

She dressed carefully, choosing the only modest dress she'd brought with her. She pulled her hair back neatly and avoided excessive makeup or jewelry, wanting to show respect to the Amish customs. Looking at herself in the mirror, she took a deep breath, hoping she was doing the right thing by thinking she could fit into his world.

The service would be held at Bishop Shetler's home, conveniently next to her grandmother's. Savannah walked, hoping the fresh air would help to clear her mind and calm her nerves.

As she approached the bishop's home, she saw a gathering of the plain-dressed congregation, which made her heart race. She scanned the crowd for Neal and spotted him near the entrance, talking to Rosalie, the rude Amish woman she'd already had a run-in with. Instantly, jealousy pricked Savannah, and those ugly, familiar tendencies rose to her chest. She took a deep breath and approached the porch, trying to suppress her feelings. Neal noticed her and broke off his conversation, walking over to greet her.

As he approached, she hoped he couldn't sense how nervous she was. "Savannah," he said softly, a genuine smile spreading across his face. "I'm glad you came."

Savannah returned his smile, though her eyes flicked to Rosalie, who was still watching them with a scowl. "I'm glad I came too." Savannah forced a smile. "I'm quite uneasy. Are you sure I'll be accepted here?" she whispered.

Before he could answer, Rosalie joined them, giving her a once-over as she approached. "I see you decided to join us today," she said, her tone not entirely welcoming.

"Yes," Savannah replied, trying to keep her voice steady. "Neal invited me."

"Well, let's hope you find what you're looking for," Rosalie said before turning away to speak with someone else.

Neal placed a reassuring hand on Savannah's elbow, leading her away. "Ignore her. She's just... protective of our ways."

Savannah nodded, feeling a surge of anger and jealousy, but determined not to let it ruin her day. "I understand."

They walked to the corner of the house where the women gathered to go in through the kitchen. The side porch was filled with Amish mothers and children, and Savannah felt their curious eyes on her. She tried to focus on the calm that seemed to permeate from Neal, who was still at her side.

Neal stopped and moved closer to whisper instructions. "This is as far as I can go with you. Just follow the women in and sit with them. I'll find you after the service."

"We can't sit together?"

"I need to sit on the men's side, and you'll be with the women. Just follow Sarah's lead. We'll meet back up after the service."

Savannah nodded, her nerves evident. Neal's eyes twinkled with mischief. "I've got a surprise for you this afternoon. Something I think you'll enjoy."

She raised an eyebrow, curiosity piqued. "A surprise, huh? You know how much I love surprises."

He chuckled softly. "I promise, it's a good one. I'll see you after the service."

With a final encouraging smile, Neal headed to the barn where the men gathered.

***

Savannah sat beside Sarah during the worship service, her nerves tingling with anticipation and uncertainty. Gigi had warned her that it would be different from anything she had attended before, but nothing could truly prepare her for this experience.

The room was filled with a quiet reverence as the congregation settled into their seats. When the three ministers stepped into the room, a silent hush fell over it, and the service began. They started singing slow and drawn-out German hymns, and the harmony of voices resonated deeply within Savannah.

At first, she just listened, absorbing the beauty of their acapella voices. Despite not understanding the words, the melodies touched her soul. Glancing over at Neal, she saw him singing along, his eyes closed and an incredible look of contentment on his face. He seemed so at peace, so connected to the moment, that she suddenly felt ill at ease.

It struck her that she'd never seen that look on him before. Was this community and lifestyle what had been missing from his life? Doubts about their marriage crept back into her mind. How could she take him away from all this? The thought of losing him filled her with dread. She knew she had to adjust to this being their new home, or she would lose the one thing that meant the most to her—Neal.

As the service continued, they started with a scripture reading. The minister's voice was calm and steady, delivering words Savannah could only catch bits and pieces of. However, she was in awe when the main message was about forgiveness and given in English.

The minister spoke about the importance of letting go of past grievances, of opening one's heart to forgive those who have wronged us. His words were simple yet profound, and they resonated deeply with Savannah. She thought about Neal's journey, his struggle for acceptance, and her battles with her parents.

A tear slipped down her cheek as she realized how much she needed to hear these words. She needed to forgive Neal, her parents, and herself. With its deep-rooted values and traditions, this community was beginning to show her a path she had never considered.

After the service, Savannah felt an internal calm she hadn't felt in years. The congregation began to mingle, and Sarah turned to her with a smile. "How did you find the service?"

Savannah took a deep breath. "It was... different, but beautiful."

***

After the service, the men lined in to share a simple meal, sitting at the long tables that had once served as church benches. The women, including Savannah, served the men before they could eat. Savannah felt a mix of nervousness and excitement as she carried a pitcher of water, making her way to Neal's table first.

He looked up at her with a warm smile as she filled his water glass. "So?" he asked, his voice filled with genuine curiosity.

Savannah smiled back, feeling a sense of connection despite the traditional setup. "It was different, but I found it beautiful. The hymns were moving, even though I didn't understand the words."

Neal nodded, understanding her sentiment. "I'd forgotten how much I enjoy them." He leaned in closer so only she could hear. "I'll translate the German words for you later."

Savannah moved down the table and found her way back into the kitchen where Sarah was.

Once the men were served, the women sat down to eat. Savannah sat beside Sarah, her guide through this new experience. The meal was simple: bean soup, homemade bread, pickles, and moon pies. Savannah found the moon pies amazing. "These are wonderful. How do you make them?" Savannah asked, savoring each bite.

Sarah smiled. "They're just dried apples, sugar, and cinnamon wrapped in pie dough. I'll teach you sometime."

The conversation flowed easily as they ate, and Savannah felt a sense of belonging growing within her. However, not everyone was as welcoming. As Savannah was helping to clear the tables after the meal, Rosalie approached her again with a sour expression.

"You think you can just walk in here and fit in?" Rosalie hissed in a low tone. "It's not that simple."

Savannah took a deep breath, remembering Sarah's advice about dealing with difficult people. "You've already made that clear. I don't expect it to be easy."

Rosalie's eyes narrowed, and she spat, "You should have never come here. You don't belong, and you'll never find your place among us."

Savannah felt a surge of anger but remembered her peace during the service. She chose her words carefully. "I'm sorry you feel that way."

After Rosalie stormed off, Savannah turned to Sarah. "How is she permitted to be so rude?"

Sarah sighed, giving Savannah a supportive nod. "She's still human with human feelings and emotions. She will have to deal with her attitude in her own time. Just remember, you can't control her reaction to you. All you can do is control your own response."

"Easier said than done," Savannah said softly.

"You will," Sarah assured her. "It takes time, and the community will come around once they learn you can be trusted to honor our ways."

As the women finished cleaning up and the men began to leave, Neal approached Savannah. "Ready to go?" he asked, his eyes filled with concern.

"Yes," she replied, forcing a smile.

They walked together, Neal's presence offering a sense of comfort. "I'm sorry about Rosalie," he said softly.

Savannah shrugged. "I just tried to be kind, like your mother and Sarah advised."

"Kindness goes a long way," Neal agreed. "Thank you for coming today. It means a lot to me."

As they walked away, Neal introduced Savannah to some community members. They were kind and welcoming, although she could sense their curiosity and perhaps a bit of skepticism.

Savannah felt mixed emotions as they walked toward the row of buggies lining the long driveway. "Thank you for inviting me, Neal. It was... different, but I think I liked it."

Savannah hesitated, then spoke. "When I first arrived, I saw you talking to Rosalie. Is there something I should know? Was she giving you a hard time about me?"

Neal stopped; his expression serious. "Rosalie and I have a complicated past. She was a friend but nothing more. She's concerned about the community and how an outsider might fit in. But you're not an outsider to me, Savannah. You're my wife, and I want us to find our way together, whatever that might look like. And I don't want you to give Rosalie a second thought. Her grievance is with me, not you."

Savannah felt a sense of relief at his words, but the jealousy still lingered. "I just…I don't want to burden you or cause you trouble."

Neal stopped in the driveway and turned her to see her eyes. "You're not a burden. You're my wife and no one and nothing is more important to me right now."

She nodded, feeling uncertain. "I hope so."

As they reached his buggy, Neal asked, "You ready for your surprise?"

"Yes," Savannah replied, her heart feeling lighter.

She let Neal take her hand to help her into the carriage. His warm touch made her heart leap at its familiarity. His fingers lingered in her hand for a few seconds before he hesitantly pulled away.

Neal smiled as he pointed to the picnic basket in the back of the buggy. "I hope you didn't overeat. I thought we'd picnic at one of my all-time favorite spots in Willow Springs."

The afternoon sun was high in the sky, adding a welcoming warmth to the fall day. Its rays danced light across Willow Creek as Neal and Savannah lingered by the water's edge. The peaceful setting distracted Savannah's churning stomach.

Neal looked around, taking in the beauty of the place that held so many memories. "I used to come here a lot when I was a kid," he began. "This was my escape, my place to think and dream."

Savannah leaned back, feeling the warmth of the sun on her face. "It's beautiful here. So peaceful."

Neal smiled, his eyes reflecting the creek. "Growing up here had challenges, but there was always a strong sense of community and faith. We didn't have much, but we had each other, and that was enough."

Savannah nodded, her thoughts drifting to her own childhood. "It sounds so different from how I grew up. My parents... they were always struggling with their own demons. I had to learn to take care of myself pretty quickly. I often felt on edge... just waiting for the next drama to unfold."

Neal reached out, patting the top of her hand. "I'm sorry you went through that, but I believe you're stronger because of it."

Savannah sighed when he quickly pulled his hand away. She stared over the water, trying to figure out if she should tell him about her pregnancy. The secret was heavy, but she decided to wait. Instead, she took a deep breath and asked, "Have you ever thought about having children?"

Neal's eyes lit up with a warmth that took Savannah by surprise. "I'd love to have a big family. I want to show my sons how to fish and farm, just like my father taught me. I hope we can live in a place much like this when I'm a father."

Savannah's heart sank a little. She wasn't sure how she would fit into the environment Neal described. "What if... what if I'm not cut out for that? I've never really thought about having children. All I ever dreamed of was having a successful career."

Neal turned toward her, his expression severe yet gentle. "What do you want now? Do you still want that career?" She watched him struggle with his next question. "Do you think you might want to move back to Charleston, or do you think you could be happy somewhere like here?"

Savannah waited a few seconds, playing with her words before responding. "Since I've been here, things have changed. I've started to see the value in a different kind of life. I want to be with you, Neal. But I don't know if I can fit into the world you're accustomed to."

Savannah took a deep breath, trying to find the right words. "Before we can even talk about those things, we need to talk about everything that's happened. The secrecy, the lies... It's been hard for me to get past all that."

Neal nodded, his eyes serious and intent. "I know I hurt you, Savannah—more than I can ever say. But I didn't lie to hurt you. I lied because I was afraid. Afraid you wouldn't accept me for who I was and afraid of losing everything we built together."

Savannah looked down, her fingers tracing patterns on the quilt they sat on. "I understand fear. But trust is so important in a marriage. How do we move forward?"

Neal reached out, gently lifting her chin so their eyes met.

Savannah sighed, her shoulders slumping. "The sermon today about forgiveness... It felt like it was directed right at me. But it's so hard to let go of the hurt."

Neal's expression softened. "Forgiveness is a process. It doesn't happen overnight. But I believe we can get there with God's help."

Savannah's voice wavered as she continued. "You said last week you needed to sort things out with God before we can move forward. What does that mean exactly? What are you hoping to figure out?"

Neal took a deep breath, gathering his thoughts. "I need to ask for forgiveness from the families of those boys, and I must make things right with God."

Neal paused, and Savannah noticed a deep crease on his brow. "I've already been to visit two of the families. One was very forgiving, yet the other could barely talk to me, let alone offer me heartfelt forgiveness."

"I bet that was hard." Savannah waited a few minutes as Neal seemed to be struggling with his own thoughts before she said, "I wish I were there for you after that visit."

"I need to face this myself, no matter how difficult."

Savannah's eyes filled with tears. "I don't know if I can handle being apart from you much longer. We should be there for each other."

Neal leaned in; his voice laced with tenderness. "This time apart isn't about separation; it's about growth. It's about us becoming the people we need to be for each other. We'll come back together stronger, more united. I promise you that."

Savannah wiped her tears, nodding slowly. "I want to believe that, Neal. I really do."

CHAPTER 14

Savannah stepped into the kitchen of the Apple Blossom Inn, the familiar hum of activity filling the air. Normally, the kitchen staff welcomed her, but today, something felt off. As she moved further into the room, she noticed the three girls huddled together, talking in hushed tones. The conversation stopped abruptly when they saw her.

The girls exchanged uneasy glances. Savannah felt a knot tighten in her stomach. She knew they were talking about her. Trying to ignore the discomfort, she approached the counter, pretending to check on the progress of the day's preparations.

The silence was apparent, and the air seemed thick with unspoken words. Old feelings of anger and distrust began to creep back into her thoughts. She had worked hard to fit into this community, but moments like this made her question if she ever truly would.

Savannah continued to her office to prepare for the upcoming festival, going over again the list of vendors. Then Mrs. Sorensen entered the room, her face tight with disapproval. Savannah looked up, surprised at the sudden tension.

"We need to talk," Mrs. Sorensen began, her voice stern.

Savannah felt a knot form in her stomach. "Of course, what's the matter?"

Mrs. Sorensen's folder her arms across her chest. "I've heard some troubling things. Word is going around that you're planning the festival according to your own ideas, disregarding my input."

"What? That's not true at all!" Savannah exclaimed, shocked. "I've been following your guidelines and incorporating the community's traditions into every aspect of the event."

Mrs. Sorensen's eyes narrowed. "Then how do you explain these rumors? I can't have someone here causing discord with the staff, especially with such an important event coming up.

Perhaps I should have gone with my gut instincts and hired someone with more knowledge of the Anabaptist community."

Savannah felt her temper rise but forced herself to stay calm. "Mrs. Sorensen, I assure you, I have the utmost respect for you and this community. I would never undermine your authority or the festival's integrity."

Mrs. Sorensen sighed, her expression softening slightly but still wary. "I don't know what to think, Savannah. This is a small town, and rumors can do a lot of damage. I can't afford to have an employee with their own agenda."

Savannah took a deep breath, her determination solidifying. "Please, give me a chance to prove myself. I'll find out who's spreading these lies and stop it. All I want is for the festival to succeed and provide our guests and those who visit the festival with a true and authentic taste of Amish country."

Mrs. Sorensen hesitated, then nodded reluctantly. "Alright, but consider this your final warning. I'll be watching closely."

Savannah nodded, feeling the weight of the situation but more determined than ever to prove herself and make the festival successful.

Later that evening, Savannah sat on the porch with Gigi, frustrated at the day's events. The sun was starting to drop behind the horizon, adding hues of pink over the fields across the road. "I can't believe this is happening, Gigi," Savannah vented. "Someone's trying to sabotage me, and Mrs. Sorensen almost fired me today because of those lies. I suspect it's Rosalie, but I can't prove anything."

Gigi rocked gently in her chair; her expression thoughtful. "I'm sorry to hear that, dear. Rosalie or not, it sounds like someone is struggling with their own insecurities. Don't let them drag you down to their level."

Savannah's anger flared, her eyes flashing. "It's not fair! I've worked so hard to fit in, to do everything right, and now someone's trying to tear me down. I'd like nothing more than to give them a piece of my mind."

Gigi reached over and placed a calming hand on Savannah's arm. "Lashing out won't solve anything. The old Savannah might have handled it that way, but you've grown so much."

Savannah took a deep breath, trying to steady her emotions. "But what can I do? I can't just let them spread lies about me."

Gigi smiled. Her eyes were full of wisdom. "Show Mrs. Sorensen and the community that you're reliable and trustworthy. Prove them wrong by your actions, not your words.

Let your honor and dedication shine through above anything else."

Savannah nodded slowly, absorbing her grandmother's wisdom. "You're right. Feeding into this drama will only make things worse. I'll focus on my work and let my actions speak for themselves."

"That's the spirit," Gigi encouraged. "Remember, integrity always wins in the end. Keep your head high and stay true to yourself."

Savannah sighed, her lingering anger still simmering beneath the surface. "It's just so hard, Gigi. I feel like I'm constantly fighting to prove myself."

"I know, dear," Gigi said softly. "But you have the strength to rise above it."

Her grandmother laughed softly. "You know your mother has gone through some of the same challenges. Sometimes, she felt she had to prove herself against gossip and a slew of lies that would have brought anyone else to their knees."

"What did she do?"

"She continued to hold her head high. It takes a lot to break your mother... you have more in common with her than you like to admit."

"I suppose so, but I can't think about that right now... I need to figure out who is trying to ruin me."

***

The next day, Savannah decided to visit Sarah. As she walked into her tidy kitchen, she marveled at how seamlessly her friend fit into motherhood. Sarah was bustling around the kitchen, preparing lunch, while her twin daughters, Emily and Hailey, played quietly at the table.

"Hey, Sarah," Savannah greeted, a touch of admiration in her voice. "You make motherhood look so easy."

Sarah laughed softly, pausing to wipe her hands on a towel. "It's far from easy, but most days, it's rewarding."

Savannah sat, watching as Sarah managed to keep an eye on the girls while finishing up the meal. The sight filled her with a mix of feelings. "Can we talk?" she asked hesitantly.

"Of course. What's on your mind?"

Savannah took a deep breath. "I'm going to be a mother. I'm terrified."

Sarah's eyes softened with understanding. "Being scared is normal. But you'll be a wonderful mother."

Savannah shook her head, her voice trembling. "I'm not so sure, and I don't want to put a child through what my mother and I've been through." She hesitated briefly before continuing. "My mother and I were inseparable once, but we've grown so distant. I never want my child to feel that void like I do."

Sarah nodded with a hint of empathy in her eyes. "But that doesn't mean you can't change. Once you become a mother, you'll understand how hard it was for your mother. And I bet you'll view your relationship differently."

Savannah felt a pang of sadness. "I don't know if my mother and I will ever be able to share that closeness again. There's so much hurt between us."

Sarah reached out and patted Savannah's hand. "You won't know until you take the first step."

As the visit continued, Savannah found herself observing Sarah with her daughters. The way Emily and Hailey clung to their mother, their giggles filling the room, stirred something deep within her. Unfamiliar longings and a desire to experience motherhood and create a bond with her child began to take root.

Savannah felt a little more at ease when she left Sarah's house. On her way home, Savannah's thoughts were consumed by her mother. She wondered how her mother would take the news of being a grandmother. Would she be happy? Supportive? Or would she be indifferent, lost in her own world as she had been for so long?

Savannah's heart ached with a deep longing. Despite all the hurt and distance, she missed her mother terribly, especially now with everything happening in her life. She wanted her mother's advice, her support, and her love. She wanted to share this monumental moment with her, to bridge the gap that had grown between them.

As she walked, memories of happier times came flooding back—times when her mother had been her best friend and confidante. They used to laugh together, share secrets, and dream about the future. But those days seemed like distant memories, overshadowed by the pain and resentment that had built up over the years.

Savannah's stomach churned with the unknown when she finally arrived at Gigi's house. She knew that reaching out to her mother would be difficult, but it was a step she needed to take. Sitting with a cup of tea, she pulled out her phone and stared at the screen, debating whether to call her. The thought of hearing her mother's voice, of possibly mending their relationship, was both terrifying and comforting.

With a deep breath, Savannah decided to take Sarah's advice to heart. She needed to try for her sake and the sake of her unborn child. She needed the courage to reach out, forgive, and heal.

Holding the phone in her hand, she whispered a silent prayer for strength and guidance. For the first time in a long while, Savannah felt a flicker of hope that she and her mother could find their way back to each other.

However, as the minutes ticked by, Savannah hesitated. She wasn't ready. Not yet. She couldn't put aside the years of hurt and resentment with one phone call. There was still so much pain to process, so much anger to let go of. She needed to think long and hard about how she really felt about mending the years of hurt she'd been harboring against both her mother and her father.

Setting the phone down, Savannah resolved to take her time. When she was truly ready, she would make that call. But for now, she needed to find peace within herself first.

***

Neal felt a pang of anger and protectiveness as he read Savannah's words. He thought about calling her, but he was honoring his father's request not to use his phone while staying with them. The frustration she described echoed his own feelings of helplessness at the severity of Savannah's plea. He knew he had to find a way to address the issues with Rosalie, not just for Savannah's sake but for the peace of their future together.

Neal,

I hope this letter finds you well. There have been rumors spreading about me at the Apple Blossom Inn, and I can't help but suspect that Rosalie is behind them. She's been causing a lot of trouble, and it's starting to affect my work and reputation with Mrs. Sorensen.

I'm not sure how to handle this situation. Confronting her directly might worsen things, and I don't want to cause any more tension in the community or between us. I need your advice and support more than ever.

I miss you and hope we can find a way through this together.

Yours always, Savannah

Neal stood in the barn, the morning light filtering through the wooden slats, highlighting the dancing dust particles in the air. The familiar smell of hay and animals brought back memories of simpler times, but the tension in the air was anything but simple with his reaction to Savannah's note. There was no denying he'd noticed how the community members looked at her, their eyes filled with doubt and suspicion. He knew his return and his marriage to Savannah did not sit well with many, including his *bruder*.

David approached; his steps heavy with purpose. Neal sensed a confrontation brewing. "We need to talk," David said, his voice low but firm.

Neal stopped and turned to face him. "Alright. What's on your mind?"

David crossed his arms, his face a mask of concern and frustration. "It's about you being here. The community isn't happy about it one bit. People are talking, and they're not saying good things. They feel Savannah's too worldly and will have too much influence over the young girls in the *g'may*. "

Neal sighed, taking in his brother's words. "Savannah would never try to persuade anyone to jump the fence. That is the furthest thing from her mind."

David's eyes narrowed. "And then there's Rosalie. I saw you talking to her the other day."

Neal's expression hardened. "David, what does my conversation with Rosalie have to do with you?"

David's jaw tightened. "You don't get it, do you? You broke her heart when you ran away. How do you expect her to act?"

Neal took a step closer, his frustration bubbling to the surface. "I'm sorry for what happened with Rosalie, but that doesn't excuse her trying to cause trouble for Savannah."

David's face flushed with anger. "Don't talk about things you don't understand."

Neal's voice was steady, but there was an edge to it. "I won't stand by and let Rosalie hurt Savannah. She's my wife, and she deserves respect."

David shook his head, frustration evident in his eyes. "And what about Rosalie? She doesn't deserve any compassion?"

Neal took a deep breath, trying to keep his emotions in check. "I understand she's hurting, but that doesn't give her the right to spread lies and create conflict."

David's shoulders slumped. "What makes you think she's causing trouble?"

Neal handed him Savannah's note. "See for yourself."

David looked down; his expression conflicted as he read Savannah's words. "You shouldn't have come back here. It would have been better for everyone if you would have just stayed away." As he turned to leave, he cast one last glance at Neal. "Just stay clear of Rosalie."

Neal watched him walk away, the silence stretching between them. But David's parting words lingered in his mind, a reminder of how much damage he'd done by leaving in the first place. He clenched his jaw, a surge of anger rising within him. He would end it if he found out Rosalie had anything to do with the rumors about Savannah.

***

Savannah's trip to the market began like any other, but she felt an inexplicable sense of unease. She pushed the feeling aside and focused on her shopping list. She couldn't shake the feeling of being watched as she navigated the crowded aisles. A different set of Amish eyes looked away at every turn, but not before glaring at her contemptuously.

Her anxiety was confirmed when she bumped into Rosalie near the produce section. Rosalie's eyes flicked over

Savannah's clothes, and a smirk curled her lips. "Still clinging to your English ways, I see," Rosalie remarked, her tone dripping with condescension.

For the first time, Savannah felt self-conscious about her attire. The jeans and sweatshirt that once made her feel confident now seemed glaringly out of place. Rosalie's words made her feel inferior, and anger rose within her. She gritted her teeth, trying to keep her calm.

"Good morning, Rosalie," Savannah said, forcing a smile. "How are you today?"

Rosalie's smirk widened. "Fine. It's nice to see you trying to fit in, even if it's not working."

Savannah swallowed her pride, remembering Gigi's advice. "It's a process, and I know acceptance won't come overnight."

Rosalie's eyes narrowed. "Some things can't be learned; some things have to be lived... something you'll never understand."

Savannah's patience was wearing thin, but she managed to nod. "You're right. But everyone has to start somewhere."

Rosalie stepped closer, her voice lowering to a more personal attack. "You know, Neal will tire of you. He might honor his marriage, but do you really think he'll be happy with his choice for the rest of his life? How does that make you feel? That your husband has to stay married to you when all along, his true desire would be to remain Amish and not straddle the fence you're forcing him to choose?"

The words stung deeply, and Savannah felt her anger flare up. But she forced herself to stay calm, though every part of her wanted to lash out. "I know Neal loves me, and I believe we'll find a way to make it work," she said, trying to keep her voice steady.

Rosalie's laugh was cold. "We'll see about that. Some things just can't be forced."

Their exchange drew the attention of others, and Savannah quickly finished shopping, trying to hold back the tears. The encounter had shaken her more than she cared to admit. For the first time, she felt the total weight of trying to fit into a community that might never fully accept her. She finished her errands quickly, feeling increasingly nauseous.

As she walked back to her car, the familiar wave of nausea hit her hard. She barely made it to the side of the parking lot before she had to stop, her stomach rebelling against the stress and frustration of the morning. So many things were much harder here in Willow Springs, and she doubted she could make the necessary changes to fit in no matter how hard she tried.

As she pulled away from the market, the struggle with her parents nipped at her heart. Instead of returning to her grandmother's, she drove towards the covered bridge, where she found solace with Neal.

Once there, she parked her car and walked along the creek path. The beauty of the surroundings offered some comfort, but her heart was heavy. She found a quiet spot by the water and fell to her knees.

"God, I don't know how to do this," she cried, tears streaming down her face. *"I don't know how to release the anger and bitterness. I don't know how to forgive my parents. But I can't keep living like this. I need Your help. Please, change my heart. Take away the bitterness and help me to forgive. Accept me as I am, broken and bitter, and make me whole again."*

She paused, taking a shaky breath. *"And Lord, please help me to see the good in Rosalie. Show me how to face what's going on between us, even when all I want to do is lash out. Following You and Your ways is hard. How do You expect me to make it?"*

She stayed there for a long time, pouring out her heart to God. She felt a sense of peace as the sun dipped lower in the sky. It wasn't an instant fix, but it was a start. She rose from her knees, feeling lighter than she had in a long time. Walking back to her car, Savannah knew she had taken the first step on a long journey. Now, she needed to trust Him to guide her through the challenges ahead. She knew it wouldn't be easy, but for the first time, she felt like she wasn't facing it alone.

As she drove back toward Gigi's, she prayed silently, *"Lord, help me trust Neal again. Show us how to honor our pasts and build a union that will work for us. Help me to forgive, truly forgive, and find peace in Your plan for our lives."*

CHAPTER 15

Neal sat on the porch, and his father joined him. He sat beside him and offered a silent moment of companionship. The quiet stretched between them, filled only with the chirping of a flock of birds settling for the night into a big pine at the edge of the side yard.

Finally, Harold broke the silence. "I've been thinking a lot about your situation with Rosalie and Savannah. It's a complicated mess, ain't so?"

Neal sighed heavily, nodding. "It sure is. I want to stay in Willow Springs but can't figure out what to do about Rosalie. I was certain she would've moved on by now, and I'm certain she's causing Savannah some undo stress."

Harold leaned back, his chair creaking softly. "David's sweet on Rosalie, you know."

"David? I didn't know, but it makes sense why he's been so on edge with me."

Harold nodded. "When the time comes, I hope you can stay here and help us run the farm, you, me, and David. But we need to figure out how Savannah fits into that picture. She might want a career, and you mentioned she might not want children. That saddens me; family means everything."

Neal looked out over the fields, lost in his own wants and desires. "I can't ask Savannah to join the Amish church; it's too much for her. There's a Mennonite church that formed in town. They hold true to many of the same values as the New Order Fellowship but don't require the dress code or the technology ban. Maybe that could be a good mix for both of us."

Harold's eyes lit up with hope. "That sounds like it could be a good fit. It's important that you both feel comfortable and connected to your faith. And if it allows you to stay here, all the better."

Neal nodded, feeling a sense of relief. "I don't care what church we attend, as long as we build our marriage on a relationship with the Lord." Neal stood and walked to the end of the porch, gathering his thoughts before continuing. "*Datt*, I want to be the godly man Savannah can be proud of and one our children can look up to as a stable family leader."

"Have you told Savannah how much children mean to you? She deserves to know how you really feel."

Neal turned to face his father; a somber look etched across his forehead. "I will. It's just hard to find the right moment. And the tension between David and me isn't helping me find my footing around here."

"Your *bruder* sees you as a threat. Perhaps he feels like he can never live up to you in Rosalie's eyes. Maybe you can find a way to help Rosalie see David differently."

"Like playing matchmaker?"

Harold didn't answer but gave him a mischievous smile.

A thoughtful plan started to form in Neal's mind. "Maybe Savannah and I can devise a way to bring them together. Help Rosalie see David for the good man he is."

"That's the spirit. There's more than one way to skin a polecat, my *datt* always said."

Neal was excited at the prospect of working with Savannah to help David and Rosalie. He stayed on the porch, eager to devise a plan as his father left to refill his coffee. Maybe he could find a way to settle this tension with David after all.

***

The following Sunday, an unexcepted warm spell settled over Willow Springs as Neal walked to join Savannah's family for dinner. The house was filled with the rich aroma of Gigi's specialty—chicken and biscuits. Savannah's father, Chad, was there too, his face lighting up with pleasure as he tasted the familiar flavors of his mother's cooking.

Savannah took a bite and savored the mouthful. "This chicken and biscuits are so good, Gigi. You really need to teach me how to make them."

After the meal, Neal and Chad moved to the front porch, and their conversation was easy and flowing. Savannah watched them from the kitchen window and couldn't help but smile. It was a rare sight to see her father so at ease and even rarer to see Neal genuinely smiling. She couldn't help but wonder what they might be discussing.

"They seem to be getting along well," Savannah remarked, her voice tinged with curiosity.

Gigi chuckled softly, a knowing smile on her face. "You do care what your father thinks, don't you? Even beneath all that tough girl front you put on."

Savannah giggled, shaking her head as she wiped down the counter. "Maybe a little. It's hard not to care when I see him like this. He seems to be enjoying Neal's company."

Gigi raised an eyebrow. "It's good to see you both more relaxed in your surroundings."

Savannah laughed, her exterior softening. "My tough girl tendencies are giving way to all this simple living."

Gigi's eyes twinkled with warmth. "It's a good change, my dear. It suits you."

Savannah's heart felt lighter as she continued cleaning. Despite all the uncertainties, moments like these made it all worthwhile. She glanced again towards the porch, feeling a small surge of hope that maybe things were falling into place.

As the sun set, Neal and Savannah took a walk. The evening air had cooled, and the peaceful surroundings made it easier for them to talk about the heavy things on their minds.

"There's something we need to talk about," Neal began, his tone severe yet gentle.

Savannah looked up at him, curious. "What is it?"

Neal sighed, kicking at a small stone on the path. "I've been having some trouble with David. He's been distant and tense around me ever since I returned. It's more than just my absence that's bothering him."

Savannah frowned. "What do you mean?"

Neal took a deep breath. "My father admitted that David has a sweet spot for Rosalie."

Savannah couldn't help but snicker. "Who could have a sweet spot for that ill-mannered, spiteful woman?"

Neal blew out a breath. "I know she's been difficult, but there's more to her than you've seen. David sees something in her, and it's causing a lot of tension between us. He thinks I'm a threat, especially since Rosalie and I have a history."

Savannah's eyebrows knitted together in concern. "What are you suggesting we do?"

"I've been thinking… what if we found a way to match the two? It might solve David's issues with me, and maybe Rosalie could see David as a suitable mate. It could bring peace to our family and help us move forward."

Savannah raised an eyebrow, skeptical. "And how do you propose we do that? It's not like we can tell them they'd be good together. That's something they need to figure out on their own."

Neal chuckled softly. "No, but we can create opportunities for them to spend time together, to see each other in a different light. It's a long shot, but it's worth trying."

Savannah pondered the idea, her mind racing with possibilities. "I suppose it couldn't hurt to try. But what if it backfires? What if Rosalie remains as spiteful as ever, and David gets hurt?"

Neal's gaze softened as he looked at her. "I believe in giving people a chance to change. Just like you've given me a chance."

Savannah felt a spark of inspiration. "I think I know how we could bring them together," she said, looking up at Neal with newfound determination.

Neal's eyes widened with curiosity. "Oh... how?"

"The Apple Butter Festival. I've been struggling to organize the apple butter making. We could ask Rosalie to supervise the process and get David to coordinate the fire. That would force them to interact with each other in a public setting."

"That's brilliant. It would allow them to spend time together without feeling forced or awkward."

"Exactly. And it's a big responsibility, something they'd both take seriously. They'd have to rely on each other, and maybe, just maybe, they'll start to see each other differently."

***

After the service at church the following Sunday, Savannah decided it was time to implement their plan. She pulled Sarah aside to discuss their plan to bring David and Rosalie together.

"Sarah, I need your help," Savannah began, explaining the situation.

Sarah listened intently and then nodded, though her face showed skepticism. "I'll talk to Rosalie. If I can convince her that we really need her help, I'm sure she'll come around. But Savannah, Rosalie isn't too fond of you running the festival. She might be resistant just because of that."

Savannah sighed. "I know, but we have to try. Maybe she'll come around if she sees it as an opportunity to contribute to the community. She certainly won't do it for me... but you might have better luck than I."

"Alright, I'll do my best."

Savannah thanked her and then turned toward Neal. "Do you think we could visit your parents' place? I'd like to ask David about keeping the fire going."

Neal smiled. "Good luck with that. As you said to Sarah, he won't do it for me but might for you."

When they arrived at the Zook farm, Neal's mother greeted them warmly, but Savannah excused herself to go to the porch to see David sitting with a book.

Savannah took a deep breath. "David, can I talk to you for a moment?" she asked, trying to keep her tone calm and friendly.

David looked up; his expression guarded. "*Jah.*"

"I need someone to coordinate keeping the fire going for the apple butter at the festival. I was hoping I could convince you to help me."

David raised an eyebrow, clearly suspicious. "That will take me away from my work for the whole day."

"Yes, and I know it's a lot to ask, especially given... well, everything. We've asked Rosalie to be in charge of making the apple butter. She has helped in previous years and knows what needs to happen."

David's stance softened slightly at the mention of Rosalie. "She agreed?"

"Not yet," Savannah admitted. "But Sarah Byler's going to talk to her. I pray she'll agree."

David looked thoughtful, then nodded slowly. "Alright, I'll do it. And don't think this means I'm not leery about you and Neal sticking around."

Savannah smiled, feeling a slight sense of accomplishment. "Thank you."

David's expression remained guarded. "Just remember, I'm doing this for the community and Rosalie. Not for you and Neal."

Savannah nodded. "I understand."

***

Savannah woke up the following day with a sharp pain in her abdomen. Panic set in immediately as she clutched her stomach, feeling an overwhelming sense of dread. She struggled to get out of bed, tears streaming down her face as she called for Gigi.

"Gigi! Help! Something's wrong!" Savannah's voice was strained and filled with fear.

Gigi rushed into the room. "Savannah, what's happening?" she asked, kneeling beside her.

"I think... I think I'm losing the baby," Savannah sobbed, clutching Gigi's hand. "The pain... "

Gigi's face went pale as she grabbed Savannah's phone and dialed 911, then explaining the situation to the dispatcher.

Within minutes, the wail of an ambulance could be heard approaching the house. Savannah's mind raced with fear, worry, and a sudden longing for Neal.

"Gigi, please call my Neal. I need him. I can't do this without him."

Gigi nodded, squeezing her hand reassuringly. "I will as soon as you're on your way."

The paramedics arrived, quickly assessing Savannah's condition and gently placing her on a stretcher. Gigi stayed close by, holding Savannah's hand until they reached the ambulance.

"I'll meet you at the hospital," Gigi promised, her voice trembling slightly.

As the ambulance doors closed, Gigi immediately called Neal, her hands shaking as she clicked through to his number on Savannah's phone. When the phone immediately went to voice mail, she scrambled to find Savannah's car keys to drive to the Zooks.

Thankfully, Neal was out by the barn and noticed her when she pulled in.

"It's Savannah. She's in an ambulance on her way to the hospital," Gigi said urgently.

Neal's heart dropped. "What happened? Is she okay?"

Gigi hesitated, knowing her condition was still a mystery to him. "She's in the family way. And she's in a lot of pain. She thinks she might be losing the baby."

"With child? Why didn't she tell me?" he muttered, his voice breaking. They rushed to the hospital, and Gigi called Chad to explain the situation on their way.

Savannah lay in the hospital bed; the sterile smell and harsh lighting amplified the emptiness she felt inside. Her heart ached with grief so deeply that she thought it might consume her.

Neal entered the room, his face etched with pain and confusion. "Why didn't you tell me?" His voice cracked with hurt.

Savannah looked away, guilt and sorrow etched on her face. "I wanted to be sure... I didn't want the baby to be the reason we tried to fix things." Tears rolled down her cheeks as she said, "I'm so sorry... I lost our baby."

Neal squeezed her hand, his eyes welling with tears, struggling to keep his voice steady. "You're okay... that's all that matters,"

Savannah took comfort in her husband's touch in the palm of her hand, her mind replaying the events of the last few hours. The sharp pain, the rush to the hospital, the helplessness as she realized she was losing the baby. There was overwhelming sadness in Neal's eyes when he found out. Until that moment, she hadn't fully grasped how much she wanted the child, how much she had already begun to love it.

"I'm so sorry. I wanted to tell you..."

Neal leaned forward, pressing his forehead against her hand. "There will be more," he whispered.

The door to her room swung open, and her father rushed in, his face pale with worry. The sight of him made Savannah's bitterness melt away in an instant. He did love her; she saw it in his eyes.

Her eyes brimmed with tears as he reached down to engulf her in a warm, tight embrace. "Oh, baby," he whispered, his voice breaking. "I'm so sorry."

Her father moved the end of the bed, his usually stoic expression softened with emotion. He gently placed his hand on her covered foot and squeezed her toes.

Savannah's own tears flowed freely as she clung to Neal's hand, feeling the weight of resentment and hurt begin to lift. She looked at her husband, the pain of her deception hanging heavily in the air. "I need to tell you something," she began, her voice barely above a whisper. "Lying here, thinking about losing this baby... all I could think about was how I didn't even share the news with you."

Neal's face crumpled, and he took her hand in both of his. "But I'm here now."

Savannah felt the lump grow as she listened to his heartfelt words. "I've been holding on to so much anger and pain," she admitted. "I felt so abandoned when you left that I wasn't sure how you would take the news." But seeing you here, rushing to my side... means everything to me. I realize now that I don't want to go through life alone. I need you by my side; please say we can be a family again."

He sighed in relief as he leaned in to kiss her forehead. "Oh, honey... I've missed you."

In that moment, surrounded by the love and support of her family, Savannah felt peace even through the loss of a child. Even the bitterness that had clouded her heart against her father began to dissolve, replaced by a newfound hope for the future.

CHAPTER 16

The early morning sun glittered across the lawn, and a cool breeze rustled a pile of leaves under the almost barren trees. Neal's decision to stay in Willow Springs and attend the Mennonite church in town had not been easy, but he felt it was the right one for him and Savannah, and he needed to discuss his plans with the bishop.

He knocked on the bishop's door with apprehension, hoping the bishop would understand and support his decision. The door opened, and Bishop Schrock's warm smile greeted him.

"Neal, come in," the bishop said, stepping aside. "I've been expecting you."

Neal followed him into the cozy living room, where they sat across from each other. The room was filled with the gentle ticking of a grandfather clock in the corner.

"Thank you for seeing me on such short notice," Neal began, his voice steady. "I've decided my future, and I wanted to discuss it with you since I've been attending a church in your district for the last month."

The bishop nodded, his eyes kind and attentive. "Of course. I'm here to listen and offer any guidance I can."

Neal took a deep breath. "Savannah and I have decided to stay in Willow Springs. We're moving into the small farmhouse next to my parents, and we plan to make it our home. We want to raise our family here, within this community. While I hate to leave the New Fellowship Church, I've also decided to attend the Mennonite church in town. I feel Savannah will adapt better there."

Bishop Schrock's expression remained thoughtful as he listened. "I see. And how does Savannah feel about this decision?"

"She's supportive," Neal replied. "We both believe it's the best path for us, and we feel it's time for us to resume as husband and wife in the eyes of the Lord."

A gentle smile spread across the bishop's face. "I know you've had your share of struggles, but it's clear that you and

Savannah are committed to building a life together here in this community."

Neal nodded, relieved that the bishop didn't try to talk him out of his decision, especially after he recommended they stay apart for some time.

"Thank you, Bishop. I want to show Savannah I can be a godly husband."

The bishop leaned back in his chair. "Being a godly husband means showing love, patience, and understanding. Savannah's spirit makes her unique, and it's important to appreciate and respect that. You'll need to balance guiding her gently and allowing her to express herself freely."

Neal listened intently, absorbing the bishop's words. "I understand. I want to be the best husband for her and our future children."

"Keep your faith strong, and always seek *Gott's* guidance. Communicate openly and work together to build a home filled with love and respect. The Mennonite church will welcome you both, and you'll find the support you need within the community."

Neal felt a weight lift off his shoulders. "Thank you. Your advice means a lot to me."

The bishop stood and placed a hand on Neal's shoulder. "Remember, marriage is a journey not without its own challenges that you'll need to cross one at a time... together."

***

After taking a few days off, Savannah woke up before dawn on the morning of the Apple Butter Festival, her chest heavy with anxiety and sorrow. The pain of losing her child was still raw, and her mind was plagued with worries about Neal's meeting with the bishop that morning. She had worked tirelessly to make this event a success, pouring her heart and soul into every detail, and today was the day everything came together. Or fell apart. Only time will tell.

She lay in bed momentarily, staring at the ceiling, wishing to pull the covers back over her head. The festival, which had once become a great distraction to her personal life, now seemed like a monumental task. Yet she knew she had to get up and face the day. Mrs. Sorensen was counting on her, and so was the community.

With a great sigh, she swung her legs over the side of the bed and stood up. She mechanically moved through her morning

267

routine, her mind drifting between the festival preparations and Neal's important meeting. What would the bishop say? Would he understand their need to shorten their time apart and look favorably at their unique situation? Could he see the sincerity in Neal's decision to withdraw from the Amish church?

As she dressed, she laid her palm on her lower tummy and choked back a lingering sob. Her hope of building a family with Neal felt distant and fragile.

As she arrived at the inn, Mrs. Sorensen was already there, overseeing the initial setup. Savannah could sense the tension in the air and knew that any slip-up could result in sharp criticism from the inn's owner.

"Morning, Mrs. Sorensen," Savannah greeted, trying to keep her tone light and positive.

"Morning, Savannah," Mrs. Sorensen replied curtly, eyes scanning the area critically. "I hope you're ready."

"I'm ready, Mrs. Sorensen. We've prepared for this, and I'm confident it will go smoothly."

Throughout the morning, the usual festival chaos began to unfold. A vendor's tent collapsed, spilling jars of apple butter onto the ground. One of the volunteers misplaced the main schedule that should have been placed at the entrance, and the weather forecast suddenly predicted rain.

Savannah took a deep breath, recalling her lessons from the Zook family and Gigi. She tackled each problem head-on, directing the volunteers calmly, finding the schedule after a frantic search, and ensuring the vendor's tent was securely reassembled.

Mrs. Sorensen observed from a distance, her critical eye not missing a thing. "Savannah, I need you to recheck the vendors," she snapped. "Make sure everything is in place. We can't afford any more mishaps."

Savannah nodded, feeling her temper rise but keeping it in check. "Yes, I'll handle it."

As the festival began, Neal arrived to help with the setup. He found a moment to pull Savannah aside, a proud smile on his face. "Everything looks perfect."

Savannah blushed, a feeling of warmth spread through her. "Thank you, Neal. I couldn't have done it without everyone's support, especially yours."

Neal looked around to ensure no one was watching them and gently rested his hand on her cheek. His eyes were filled with love and hope. "You're doing great," he said.

Their tender moment was abruptly interrupted by Rosalie, who approached with a scowl. "Seems like you have everything under control, Savannah," she said sarcastically.

Savannah took a deep breath, remembering Gigi's advice to rise above the pettiness. "Thank you."

Before Rosalie could respond, David walked up, immediately calming her. "Rosalie, can you show me where you want me to stack more wood?"

Rosalie's demeanor softened, and she nodded. "Of course, I'll be right there."

As they walked away, Savannah and Neal exchanged glances, noting the change in both Rosalie and David. Their plan to bring them together seemed to be working.

The festival continued smoothly, Savannah managing each challenge with newfound confidence and grace. Mrs. Sorensen hovered nearby, her critical eye always watching, but Savannah remained unfazed.

***

The day had been a whirlwind of activity, but everything was going smoothly by mid-afternoon. The vendors were happy, the community was engaged, and Savannah felt a sense of pride and accomplishment as she watched families enjoy the festival. It seemed like nothing could go wrong.

Savannah was overseeing the apple butter-making station when she heard a loud scream followed by panicked shouts. Her heart skipped a beat as she turned towards the commotion. Neal was by her side instantly.

"What's happening?" Savannah asked, her voice trembling.

Neal pointed to the source of the chaos. "Fire!"

Savannah's eyes followed his gesture, and her heart sank. Flames were billowing out of the Apple Blossom Inn's roof. Thick black smoke curled into the sky, and the scent of burning wood filled the air. Panic spread quickly among the festivalgoers as they realized the gravity of the situation.

"Everyone, stay calm!" Neal shouted, trying to take control of the situation. "We need to make sure everyone gets out safely."

Savannah's mind raced. "We have to help," she said, her voice resolute.

Neal nodded, squeezing her hand briefly before they both sprang into action. Savannah ran towards the inn, where Mrs. Sorensen frantically directed people out of the building.

"Mrs. Sorensen!" Savannah called, rushing to her side. "Is everyone out?"

"I don't know," Mrs. Sorensen replied, her face pale with fear. "I can't find the kitchen staff."

Neal stepped forward. "I'll check," he said firmly.

"Neal, be careful," Savannah called after him, her heart pounding as he disappeared into the smoke-filled building.

Savannah stood outside, her heart in her throat, praying fervently for Neal's safety. The heat was intense, and the smoke made it difficult to see. She could hear the fire's crackling and the firefighters' shouts as they arrived and began their work.

Minutes felt like hours as Savannah waited, her eyes never leaving the inn's entrance. Suddenly, she saw movement through the smoke. Neal emerged, supporting two kitchen staff and helping them to safety.

Relief washed over Savannah, and she ran to him as he brought them out into the fresh air. Neal was coughing, his face streaked with soot, but he was unharmed.

"Are you okay?" she asked, her voice shaking.

Neal nodded, though his breathing was labored. "I'm fine. We got everyone out."

Firefighters continued their work, battling the blaze that consumed the roof. Savannah watched in dismay, feeling a hand on her shoulder. She turned to see Mrs. Sorensen, with tears in her eyes.

"Thank you, Neal," Mrs. Sorensen said, her voice choked with emotion. "You saved lives today."

Neal shook his head. "We all did our part. I'm just glad everyone is safe."

As the firefighters worked to control the fire, Savannah felt a wave of exhaustion. She leaned against Neal, who wrapped his arm around her, offering silent support.

The festival, which had started as a celebration, had become a test of their community's spirit. Savannah was determined to rise to the occasion, no matter what lay ahead.

But as the evening wore on, murmurs began to spread through the crowd. Someone claimed to have seen Neal behind the inn shortly before the fire started. The fire chief conducted a preliminary investigation and declared that the fire had been started deliberately. Wood embers had been dumped alongside the back wall, igniting the old wooden siding. Whispers and suspicious glances were directed at Neal throughout the gathered crowd.

The following day, Savannah and Neal sat silently in their kitchen. The peace of the previous day had evaporated, replaced by a heavy tension.

"I can't believe they think you did it," Savannah said, her voice breaking. "You saved people; you were a hero."

Neal's expression was grim. "Someone's trying to force us out of Willow Springs. I don't know who, but we must find out who and why." Before they could discuss it further, there was a knock on the door. Savannah opened it to find two men standing there, one holding a badge.

"Detective Powers, Willow Springs Police Department," the man said. "This is my partner, Detective Harris. We must ask you a few questions about yesterday afternoon's fire."

Neal invited them in, his face pale but determined. "Of course. Ask anything you need."

They sat at the kitchen table, and the detectives began their questioning.

"Mr. Zook, where were you when the fire started?" Detective Powers asked.

"I was helping at the apple butter-making station," Neal replied calmly. "When we heard the commotion, I ran inside to find the kitchen staff."

"We've had reports that you were seen behind the inn shortly before the fire started," Detective Harris added, his tone accusatory.

Neal shook his head. "That's not true. I was never behind the inn."

Savannah's anger flared. "Who said they saw him? This is ridiculous. Neal would never do something like this."

"We can't disclose our sources," Detective Powers said. "But we need to investigate every lead."

The questioning continued for what felt like hours. Finally, the detectives left, leaving Neal and Savannah more isolated than ever.

"We'll prove them wrong," Neal said, his voice steady. "We'll find out who's behind this."

Savannah nodded. The suspicion and distrust from the community were painful, and she couldn't shake the feeling that their peaceful life in Willow Springs was being torn apart.

***

As the investigation continued, Neal and Savannah became outcasts in the community they had grown to love. People on the street ignored them, turning away when they passed by. The friendly smiles and waves they had started to receive were replaced with cold stares and whispered conversations.

Savannah felt the weight of the suspicion and mistrust deeply. The stress began to take a toll on her, both emotionally and physically. She spent more time indoors, avoiding the judgmental eyes of the townspeople. Her once vibrant energy was replaced with a deep sadness, and Neal watched helplessly as the light in her eyes dimmed.

One evening, after another day of being shunned by the community, Savannah sat on the porch, tears streaming down her face. Priscilla found her there, rocking gently in her chair.

"Priscilla, I don't know how much more of this I can take," Savannah confessed, her voice breaking. "It feels like the whole world is against us."

Priscilla placed a comforting hand on Savannah's shoulder. "I know it's hard, my dear. But remember, God can find beauty in the ashes of any situation. You and Neal must stay strong, not just for yourselves, but for each other and your future."

Savannah nodded, wiping her tears. "But how do we do that when everyone believes these horrible lies about us?"

Priscilla smiled gently. "By showing them the truth through your actions. The community is watching how you respond to this negativity. If you crumble, they'll believe the worst. But if you stand strong and show grace, even in the face of adversity, they'll see the strength of your character and your faith."

Neal joined them on the porch, hearing the tail end of their conversation. He took Savannah's hand, squeezing it gently. "*Mamm's* right. We can't let this break us. We must show everyone we won't be forced from our home or community."

As the days passed, Neal and Savannah made a conscious effort to stay involved in the community. They continued to attend church services, participate in community events, and help wherever they could. Despite the cold shoulders and harsh whispers, they remained steadfast.

***

Winter had started to grip November, and Savannah found herself sweeping dirt from the sidesteps when she heard a voice behind her. She turned to see Sadie Beiler, one of the girls from the kitchen at the Apple Blossom Inn, standing nervously at the garden's edge.

"Sadie, it's good to see you," Savannah said, brushing the dirt to the ground.

Sadie stepped closer; her face filled with concern. "Savannah, I need to talk to you about the fire."

Savannah felt her heart skip a beat. "What is it, Sadie?"

Sadie glanced around. "I've heard people saying that Neal started the fire, but I know that's not true. I saw someone else before the fire started."

Savannah's eyes widened. "You did? Who was it?"

Sadie shook her head. "I don't know his name, but he was tall, with brown hair much like Neal, but it wasn't your husband. I saw him out the kitchen window just before the fire broke out."

Savannah felt a surge of hope. "Thank you for telling me, Sadie. This could help clear Neal's name."

Sadie nodded. "I just wanted to do what's right. I hope it helps."

***

As the days passed, Sadie's information renewed hope in Neal and Savannah. They were determined to find out who was behind the fire and clear Neal's name. Neal decided it was time to speak with Bishop Weaver one crisp morning. He hoped the Old Order bishop might have some insight into the rumors and help them navigate through the tangled web of suspicion. Neal and Savannah prayed together for strength and guidance before he set out on his quest.

The old man sat on the porch as Neal approached. The bishop looked up and smiled warmly as Neal approached.

"Neal, it's good to see you," Bishop Weaver greeted him. "What brings you here today?"

Neal took a deep breath, trying to steady his nerves. "Bishop Weaver, I need to talk to you about the fire at the Apple Blossom Inn. Rumors have been circulating about my involvement, and I need to find out who is spreading these lies. I figured you'd know more than anyone else in this community."

The bishop's expression turned serious as he gestured for Neal to sit down. "I've heard some of the talk. It's troubling, to say the least."

Neal leaned forward. "I need to know who might be behind these rumors. I want to clear my name and find out who would want to see Savannah and I driven out of Willow Springs."

Bishop Weaver took a sip from his cup, deep in thought. "Rumors can spread like wildfire in a close-knit community like ours. I've heard a few names mentioned, but I can't say for certain who's responsible."

Neal's heart sank slightly, but he pressed on. "One of the girls from the kitchen told Savannah she saw someone before the fire started. We need to get to the bottom of this."

The bishop's eyes narrowed as he considered Neal's words. "People in the district have been vocal about their feelings towards you and Savannah. I hope the members under my care wouldn't contribute to the Amish grapevine, but I'm not blind to see how a few bad seeds can hurt a good harvest."

Neal nodded, appreciating the bishop's honesty. "Is there anyone you can think of who might have a reason to spread these lies?"

Bishop Weaver sighed. "In a community like ours, jealousy and resentment don't creep in often without me knowing. It could be anyone, especially knowing how you've stirred up things around here again. I'll keep my ears open and see what I can find out."

"Savannah and I just want to clear my name and move forward. We don't want to cause any more trouble."

The bishop nodded. "The truth will come to light... it always does."

CHAPTER 17

The weeks following the fire investigation were chaotic for Neal and Savannah. Despite their efforts to uncover the truth, more damaging evidence surfaced, further implicating Neal. The whispers grew louder, and the tension in Willow Springs was obvious wherever they went. Determined to clear Neal's name, Savannah decided to confront Rosalie directly. She needed to know if Rosalie harbored lingering grudges that might have driven her to such lengths.

On a brisk afternoon with snow in the forecast, Savannah made her way to Rosalie's home. The walk gave her time to gather thoughts and steady herself for the confrontation. When she arrived, Rosalie answered the door with a look of surprise.

"Savannah," Rosalie greeted, her tone cautious.

Savannah took a deep breath, trying to keep her voice steady. "I need to talk to you. Can I come in?"

Rosalie stepped aside, allowing Savannah to enter. They settled in the sparse living room, their tension almost tangible.

"I need to know if you had anything to do with the rumors about Neal and the fire," Savannah began, her voice firm but pleading. "This has caused so much pain for both of us, and I have to get to the bottom of it."

Rosalie's expression hardened. "You think I would do something like that? Sabotage Neal and spread lies?"

Savannah met her gaze, trying to read her emotions. "I don't know what to think anymore. But I need to hear it from you."

Rosalie's defiance softened slightly. "Savannah, I cared deeply for Neal once. Yes, I was hurt when he left, but I would never do something so underhanded. I wouldn't jeopardize my standing in the community, let alone hurt someone I once cared for." Rosalie sighed. "I'm not going to lie. I was the one who spread rumors about you to Mrs. Sorensen, but I would never hurt Neal."

Savannah felt a flicker of hope. "If not you? Who would want to harm Neal?"

Rosalie sighed, frustration evident in her voice. "I don't know. But I can tell you one thing—my affections have shifted. David and I have been spending time together, and I wouldn't risk that for anything."

Savannah's eyebrows raised in feigned surprise. "You and David?"

Rosalie nodded, a hint of a smile playing on her lips. "Yes, we're becoming friends. I wouldn't jeopardize that relationship by stirring up trouble for his *bruder*."

Savannah's mind raced. If Rosalie wasn't behind the rumors, who could be? "Thank you, Rosalie," Savannah said, her voice sincere. "I appreciate your honesty."

Rosalie stood to show her to the door. "I hope you and Neal can clear this up." Rosalie walked to the door and paused momentarily. "I'm sorry for how I've treated you. You didn't deserve it, and I hope you can forgive me."

"I hope we can be friends one day, and of course, you're forgiven." Savannah even surprised herself with her quick response.

As Savannah left Rosalie's home, she felt strange emotions. While she was relieved that Rosalie wasn't behind the rumors, the mystery of who was trying to sabotage them remained unsolved. The sun was starting to set as she walked along the gravel road back home to the tiny *doddi haus* next to Neal's parents, her thoughts a whirlwind of possibilities.

Her footsteps echoed softly in the twilight, the chilly evening air brushing against her face. As she neared the edge of the woods, she heard a rustle in the underbrush. Savannah paused, her heart pounding as she strained to see through the dim light.

"Hello?" she called out.

There was no response, just the sound growing closer. Suddenly, someone rushed her from behind, a strong arm wrapping around her waist, another clamping over her mouth. Savannah struggled, trying to scream, but her cries were muffled. Panic surged through her as she was pulled into the weeds, the world around her blurred.

She fought with all her might, kicking and thrashing, but her attacker was too strong. Her heart raced, terror gripping her as she realized the seriousness of her situation. Desperation set in, her thoughts racing to Neal, to her family, to the baby she lost.

The man dragged her deeper into the woods, and Savannah's mind spun with fear and confusion. Who could be doing this? And why? She tried to remember everything her mother had taught her about staying calm in a crisis, but it was difficult with the adrenaline coursing through her veins.

As they stopped in a small clearing, the man released his hold on her, shoving her to the ground. The lingering smell of sweat and stale alcohol penetrated the air as she gasped for a breath. He placed a heavy boot on her back as she turned her face toward him; she saw a quick glimpse of his face in the fading light. His eyes glowed like fire as she closed her own, praying for anything to get her out of this situation.

***

Neal had been restless since his conversation with Savannah. The more he thought about it, the more convinced he became that Rosalie's past feelings for him might have played a role in the recent troubles. But it wasn't just about Rosalie—he also needed to confront David.

Neal decided it was time to address his suspicions. He found his *bruder* in the barn, working on a buggy. The air was thick with hay and the faint smell of manure. Neal took a deep breath and approached David.

"David," Neal said, his voice steady but tense.

David looked up; his expression wary. "What? Can't you see I'm busy?"

Neal stepped closer; his eyes locked onto his *bruder's.* "I need to know if Rosalie had anything to do with the fire and if you're involved somehow."

David's expression turned to anger. "You think I had something to do with that?"

Neal's jaw tightened. "I don't know what to think. But the rumors are spreading, and someone is trying to force us away from here, and you're the only one I know who seems to have a beef with us."

David slammed a wrench down onto the workbench, his face flushed with fury. "You have some nerve accusing me. After I've spent the last six years defending you." David pushed by him to pick up another tool. "And this is the thanks I get?"

Neal's anger flared. "I'm trying to make things right! But I can't do that if someone is sabotaging my efforts."

The argument swelled, their voices rising, the tension between them escalating, and it wasn't long before Harold heard the commotion and came rushing into the barn.

"What's going on here?" Their father demanded, stepping between the two of them.

Neal and David tried to speak simultaneously, their words tumbling over each other in a heated clash. Harold held up his hand, silencing them.

"One at a time," Harold said sternly, his eyes flashing with disappointment.

Neal took a deep breath, his anger simmering just below the surface. "I suspect Rosalie might be involved in the rumors about the fire, and I needed to confront David about it."

David's eyes blazed with resentment. "And he thinks I'm in on it too. Can you believe that?"

Harold looked between his sons, his expression hardening. "This has gone too far. I won't have this kind of discord in our family. Neal, you can't go around making accusations without proof. And David, you need to understand the pressure Neal's under."

David crossed his arms, his anger giving way to a grudging understanding. "I get that, but accusing me of something like this? That's crossing a line."

Neal took a step back, his anger deflating. "I just need to know the truth, David. I'm trying to protect my family."

Harold placed a hand on each of their shoulders, his grip firm. "This bickering needs to stop. We must work together to find out who's behind this, not tear each other apart."

Neal nodded, his frustration giving way to a weary determination. "You're right."

Harold sighed, relieved to see the tension easing. "Good. Now, let's get back to work. We have much to do and can't afford to be divided."

Neal felt a momentary sense of relief, but his frustration quickly returned. He turned on his heel and stormed out of the barn, needing to clear his head. David's voice echoed behind him as he walked away, filled with bitterness and hurt.

"There you go again, running away when things get tough. You'll never change."

Neal paused momentarily, his back to David, feeling the weight of his brother's words. Without turning around, he continued walking, the sting of David's accusations burning deep. He needed to find a way to stand his ground and show everyone, including David, that he was there to stay.

***

The sun dipped below the horizon as Neal paced the porch, worry etched deeply on his face. Savannah wasn't home, and he had no idea where she might have gone. As darkness settled in, his anxiety grew. He couldn't shake the feeling that something was terribly wrong.

After what felt like an eternity, he decided he couldn't wait any longer. He grabbed his coat and headed toward David's house, his heart heavy with regret for their earlier argument. As he approached, he saw David through the window, sitting at the kitchen table with Rosalie and her younger *schwester*. Taking a deep breath, he knocked on the door.

David opened it, his expression wary. "Neal?"

"I need your help," Neal said, his voice strained with worry. "Savannah isn't home, and I have no idea where she might have gone. I'm worried something might have happened to her."

Rosalie responded quickly. "I saw her a couple of hours ago. She stopped by my parent's house to ask if I had anything to do with the fire."

"Did she say where she might be going?"

"No, but she headed back toward your house, so I assumed she was going home."

David and Rosalie stood up, concern flashing across their faces as they said in unison. "What can we do?"

Neal nodded. "I need your help looking for her. This is not like her, and I can't help but think she's in trouble."

David's face softened as he grabbed his hat and jacket off the peg by the back door.

Together, they quickly spread the word among the neighbors. The community, despite their recent suspicions and gossip, rallied together. Lanterns and flashlights flickered to life as groups of people set out to search the surrounding areas, calling out Savannah's name into the night.

Neal and David checked every possible place, up and down Willow Bridge Road and in the nearby woods, asking everyone they encountered if they had seen her. The night air grew colder, and Neal's worry deepened each minute.

Hours passed, and the search party grew weary but determined. Neal's heart ached with each step, fearing the worst but hoping for the best. He couldn't lose Savannah, not now, not after everything they had been through.

Just as the night seemed darkest, a shout rang out from the edge of the woods. "Over here! I found something!"

Neal's heart raced as he and David ran toward the voice. They found old man Yoder holding up a piece of fabric that Neal recognized as part of Savannah's jacket.

"She must be nearby," Mr. Yoder said, his voice steady despite the urgency in his eyes.

The search party fanned out with renewed energy, calling Savannah's name louder. But despite their efforts, there was no other sign of her. Panic gripped Neal's heart tighter as morning light trickled above the horizon.

As he returned to his house to regroup and contemplate calling in a missing person's report, he stopped cold when a message was pinned to his front door. MISSING SOMEONE? NOW YOU KNOW HOW IT FEELS.

Neal's blood ran cold. He knew exactly who had written the note. Jacob Miller, Joe's younger *bruder*. He couldn't believe that Jacob had harbored such hatred for so long. Neal didn't hesitate; he grabbed the note and ran to the barn, leaving only a brief explanation to his father and brother. He knew exactly where to find Savannah. His father owned the harness shop just down the road and close to Rosalie's parents' house.

When Neal arrived, he found Jacob holding Savannah, bound and gagged, her eyes wide with fear. Jacob's face was twisted with rage and grief.

"Took you long enough," Jacob yelled.

Savannah's muffled sob rang in his ears as he stood in the doorway.

"Let her go," Neal demanded. "This is between you and me."

"How does it feel to miss someone you care about?" Jacob spat. "I should have led little Miss City Girl to the same death, but I wanted to see the fear in your eyes face to face."

Neal stepped forward; his hands raised. "I know you're angry, and I'm sorry. But this won't bring Joe back. Hurting Savannah won't make things right."

Jacob's grip on Savannah tightened, and she winced under his hold. "You don't get to tell me what's right and wrong."

Neal's heart pounded. He had to keep Jacob talking to find a way to get Savannah to safety. "I'm ready to face the consequences of my actions. But Savannah is innocent in all this. Let her go, and we can talk."

Jacob's eyes flickered with uncertainty, and Neal noticed the slight sway in Jacob's stance at that moment of hesitation. He could smell the alcohol on his breath. Neal's mind raced, trying to find a way to exploit Jacob's impaired state.

"Jacob, Joe was my friend too. I've lived with more guilt than you can imagine," Neal's voice cracked with genuine emotion. "But this isn't the answer. We both know it."

Jacob's grip loosened slightly, confusion mingling with the rage in his eyes. "You don't know anything," he muttered, but his voice lacked conviction.

Neal took a step closer. "Joe wouldn't want this. He wouldn't want you to ruin your life over this."

Seeing his chance, Neal lunged forward, knocking Jacob off balance. The two men struggled fiercely, but Neal's desperation and determination gave him the strength to overpower Jacob.

Wrestling each other in a battle of strength, Jacob's voice was filled with a crazed murmur of rants. "You think it was all you? Don't you? Well, let me tell you, you're not the only one who has demons to face. I was the one who drove them deeper into the woods after you left. It was me! It was me, and I let you take the blame!"

Suddenly, everything made sense, and Neal's mind raced as he relived those last few moments six years ago. He had given the three boys plenty of ways to find their way out of the deep thicket he had led them to. He abruptly realized the depth of Jacob's torment and the twisted guilt that had driven him to take his shame out on Savannah.

Finally, with a surge of strength, Neal knocked Jacob back hard enough to free himself from their entanglement. He quickly picked Savannah up and headed to the door, her sobs of relief mingling with his heavy breathing.

Running from the shop, leaving Jacob dazed, they made it to the edge of the road, where a line of buggies had made their way to the parking lot to the harness shop.

Setting Savannah down, he untied her hands and removed the rag from her mouth. Jacob's distant, crazed shouts could still be heard as he pulled her into his arms.

"I was so scared," she mumbled as she buried her face in his chest.

"It's over now." He managed to say with an edge of assurance. "You're safe now."

Savannah nodded, tears streaming down her face. "He admitted that he had started the fire. He wants you to hurt as much as he does," she whispered.

"I'm so sorry," he breathed, holding her tighter.

Neal looked at his father. Overcome with emotion, Neal took a moment before repeating what Jacob had admitted to. "*Datt*, Jacob drove those boys deeper into the woods. It wasn't my fault they died." A stunned silence fell over his father as they all absorbed Jacob's confession. Neal's eyes filled with tears.

Neal felt a rush of conflicting emotions. Anger, relief, and a profound sadness mingled within him. "He let me carry that burden for years. I believed it was all my fault." The weight of the past suddenly felt different, lighter, yet more complex. Neal turned to Savannah, who still had tears in her eyes.

"I'm so sorry, Neal," she whispered, her voice filled with empathy.

Neal pulled her into a tight embrace, finding comfort in her presence. "It wasn't just me," he said, his voice trembling. "All this time, it wasn't just me."

The community members around them shared somber glances, the truth settling in. The healing process had only begun, but Neal felt like the truth had finally set him free for the first time in years.

CHAPTER 18

In the months following the harrowing events, the community rallied around Mrs. Sorensen to rebuild the Apple Blossom Inn. The fire had left a gaping hole in Willow Springs. Still, the Amish community, known for their resilience and unity, united with a collective determination to restore and improve the beloved landmark.

Neal took it upon himself to organize the rebuilding efforts, working tirelessly to coordinate the many hands eager to help. He saw it as an opportunity to give back to the community that had shown them support and prove that he and Savannah could be integral members of the Amish community, even if they chose to remain *Englisch*.

Early one morning, as the first beams were raised, the hum of activity filled the air. The Amish men, skilled in carpentry and construction, worked seamlessly, their expertise evident in every precise cut and measured placement. The women, including Priscilla and Gigi, prepared meals and provided support, their nurturing presence keeping spirits high and stomachs full.

Savannah, though still recovering from the emotional and physical strain of her kidnapping, insisted on being part of the effort. She found solace in the work and felt a renewed sense of purpose. Despite her background, the community's acceptance of her was a testament to their forgiving nature and desire to see her and Neal thrive.

One afternoon, as Savannah was painting a new section of the inn's exterior, Mrs. Sorensen approached her, wiping her hands on her apron.

"You've done a remarkable job, Savannah," she said, her tone softer than usual.

Savannah smiled, her heart warming at the unexpected praise. "Thank you, Mrs. Sorensen. It means a lot coming from you."

Mrs. Sorensen nodded, her stern demeanor giving way to a hint of a smile. "You and Neal have proven yourselves. The community respects hard work and integrity; you've shown both in abundance."

Neal, overhearing the conversation, joined them. "We couldn't have done it without everyone's help. It's been an incredible experience."

Mrs. Sorensen glanced around at the bustling activity. "The inn will be better than ever, thanks to all of you."

As the weeks turned into months, the Apple Blossom Inn took shape, more magnificent than before. The new design included additional rooms and a larger dining area, improvements that would allow Mrs. Sorensen to accommodate more guests and host bigger events. And, with the upcoming launch of her Amish Bake Off, the new space will be needed more than ever. The community's pride in their work was evident, and a sense of accomplishment permeated the air.

The entire community gathered to celebrate on the day of the grand reopening. Savannah stood beside Neal, her hand in his, as Mrs. Sorensen cut the ribbon. Cheers erupted, and everyone shared the joy of the moment.

Neal turned to Savannah, his eyes reflecting his love and admiration for her. "We did it."

Savannah squeezed his hand, her heart full but with a lingering weight. "Yes, we did, but I think there is still one more thing I must do."

Neal looked at her with understanding and nodded. "Go on. I'll be right here."

Savannah stepped away from the crowd and found a quiet spot under a large oak tree. She took a deep breath and pulled out her phone, her fingers trembling slightly as she dialed her mother's number. The phone rang twice before her mother answered.

"Hello?" her mother's voice sounded tentative, unsure.

"Mom, it's me, Savannah," she said, her voice thick with emotion.

There was a pause, and Savannah could almost hear the surprise and hope in her mother's silence. "Savannah, it's so good to hear your voice."

Savannah's eyes filled with tears. "Mom, I... I've been thinking a lot about us. About everything that happened and how we drifted apart."

Her mother's voice trembled. "I've missed you so much, Savannah. I know I've made mistakes, and I'm so sorry for all the hurt I caused you."

Savannah wiped a tear from her cheek. "I know, Mom. And I'm sorry too. I've been carrying so much anger and bitterness, and it's been eating away at me. I realize now that holding onto all that pain hasn't done either of us any good."

Her mother's sobs were audible through the phone. "I wish I could go back and change things, but all I can do is hope we can start fresh."

Savannah's voice softened. "I want that too, Mom. I want to let go of the past and build something new with you. Can we do that?"

"Yes, sweetheart, we can," her mother replied, her voice filled with relief and love.

They spent the following few minutes sharing memories, laughing, and crying together. Savannah felt a sense of peace and closure for the first time in years. She knew this was the beginning of a new chapter in their relationship.

As she hung up the phone, Neal walked over to her, wrapping his arms around her. "How did it go?" he asked gently.

Savannah looked up at him, her eyes shining with hope. "It went well. Better than I could have imagined. I feel like a huge weight has been lifted off my shoulders."

Neal kissed her forehead. "I'm so proud of you, Savannah. You've come such a long way."

Savannah rested her head against his chest. "Thank you for always being there for me. I couldn't have done this without you."

Savannah felt a deep sense of gratitude and love as they stood there, holding each other under the oak tree. She knew that with Neal by her side and her relationship with her mother on the mend, there was nothing she couldn't face. Together, they would continue to build a life filled with love, forgiveness, and hope.

Savannah pulled back slightly, looking up at Neal with a soft smile. "There's something else I need to tell you."

Neal raised an eyebrow, curiosity lighting his eyes. "What is it?"

She took his hand and laid it on her tummy, her voice trembling with emotion. "And I can't imagine going through it without my whole family. You, Dad, Gigi, and... of course, Mom."

Neal's eyes widened, filling with tears of joy. "Savannah, that's amazing news!"

Savannah nodded, her own tears spilling over. "I'm scared, but I'm also hopeful. I want our child to grow up surrounded by love and family."

Neal pulled her close, continuing to rest his hand gently on her stomach. "We'll do it together. This time, we'll have everyone we love supporting us. Our family will be stronger than ever."

As they embraced, the warmth of the afternoon sun enveloped them, and Savannah felt a renewed sense of peace. With Neal's love, her family's support, and a newfound connection to her mother, she knew they could face any challenge ahead. Their future was bright, filled with love, forgiveness, and the promise of new beginnings.

EPILOGUE

A year had passed since the Apple Blossom Inn was rebuilt, and the bustling streets of Willow Springs were now filled with a new sense of community. Now a mother, Savannah embraced the simplicity and richness that had once felt so foreign to her.

Today was a special day. Savannah left their daughter, Aubrey, at Gigi's house so she and Neal could attend David and Rosalie's wedding. As she handed the baby swing to Gigi, she noticed her father sitting on the porch with an old friend. The joy in his eyes was unmistakable, and Savannah couldn't help but smile at the sight.

"Looks like Dad's found happiness again," Savannah said, her voice filled with warmth.

Gigi nodded, her eyes twinkling. "Yes, he has. Love has a way of finding us, even when we least expect it."

Savannah watched as her father laughed with his childhood sweetheart, a woman who was no longer Amish but was definitely still in love with him. It had been years since she had seen him so happy.

Savannah's mother showed up as they were about to leave for the wedding. Her face lit up with a genuine smile, and she warmly greeted them. The past year proved that forgiveness could heal not only Savannah's family but also Neal's.

"Mom, it's so good to see you," Savannah said, embracing her mother. Her mother returned the hug, her eyes glistening with tears.

"Thank you for coming to help Gigi with the baby. It means a lot to me."

Her mother smiled, her gaze softening. "I wouldn't miss it for the world. I hope there'll never come a time when you and Aubrey are at odds."

Savannah laughed with a lightness in her heart. "I hope not, but I am a product of my mother and can still be difficult if pushed too hard... ask Neal."

Her mother chuckled, brushing a strand of hair from Savannah's face. "Don't be too hard on your children and enjoy being a mother. You're doing an amazing job, and I see how you've overcome your past. You're not letting your father's and my mistakes define who you want to be."

Savannah's eyes filled with gratitude. "Thank you, Mom. That means everything to me."

They stood there momentarily, the past's wounds healing in the light of their newfound understanding and love. The sound of laughter and joy from the living room as Gigi cooed over the baby reminded Savannah of the beautiful life they were all building together.

Savannah glanced over at her parents, now chatting amicably on the porch. She teased them both. "It's good to see you and Dad can be in the same room together and be friends."

Her mother nodded, a wistful smile on her face. "We've both grown a lot, and forgiveness has played a big part. I'm glad we can all be here for each other now."

As Savannah and Neal prepared to leave for the wedding, she felt a deep sense of peace. The past year had been a journey of forgiveness and healing, and she was ready to embrace the future with an open heart, surrounded by the love of her family and community.

***

Read more in the seventh book of
The Amish Women of Lawrence County Series.
<u>*Ruth's Amish Words of Faith*</u>

When Ruth Yoder and Wilma Nettles face one of life's most challenging circumstances, they find solace and laughter in an unlikely friendship. Ruth, a devout Amish woman, and Wilma, a spirited English woman, both receive a severe diagnosis that brings them together in a way neither could have imagined.

Ruths

AMISH WORDS OF FAITH
THE AMISH WOMEN OF
LAWRENCE COUNTY SERIES - BOOK 7

Tracy Fredrychowski

PROLOGUE

I'll never forget the chill of that sterile room as I sat waiting for the doctor to read my scans. The technicians' murmur left me feeling nervous as they retook images with precise care. A million thoughts were floating around in my head, but none stronger than the thought of my grandchildren possibly not having their *grossmommi* to see them to adulthood. And then there was Levi, who was waiting for me just behind the closed doors. How would he fair without me?

His strong presence that day was the only thing that kept me from breaking down into tears. That and showing emotion in such a public place would show a weakness I wasn't ready to share with strangers.

After the tests were completed, the nurse instructed me to return to the waiting room and wait for the doctor to call us back into his office. As I walked to find Levi, I wondered how we'd overcome such a challenge.

I had just celebrated my sixtieth birthday, and I was now facing a life-altering health diagnosis that would possibly change the lives of my family and myself forever. Nothing made sense as I pushed through the double doors to find my husband's comforting presence.

Sitting beside Levi, he gave me a warm smile, but we remained quiet. The waiting room was filled with people of all ages and levels of care. Many were thin and sickly looking, but some were full of life, laughing and chatting like they had known each other for years. The whole scene left me brushing away my thoughts that the waiting room reeked of death, and I wanted to be anywhere but here. Noting their smiling faces left me ashamed of my worrisome thoughts, and I struggled to push fear from my mind. Concentrating instead on the things I could control.

Levi and I were completely out of our element. Besides a few friendly nods, most *Englischers* in the waiting room ignored us and left us to our thoughts. The room was cold, and I snuggled as close as I could to the warmth of Levi's arm, which he purposely moved closer when he caught me pulling my sweater tighter.

We didn't need words or outward touch, as our eyes and closeness spoke of our undying love for one another. Levi... my rock and the man *Gott* had so graciously paired me with, was my silent giant.

The heaviness in the air was almost suffocating, and I felt myself closing my eyes. In an instant, the image of my mother came to mind. A small part of me yearned for her even though I knew how silly it was since she'd been gone for many years. But when times like this come up quickly, there's a sense of comfort in wanting to talk through a stressful situation with your mother.

I longed to hear her voice, to feel her comforting embrace, to have her tell me everything would be alright. But instead, I sat in silence, my heart aching with the weight of my fears. Levi's hand quickly found mine, squeezing gently before pulling it away, a silent promise that we would face this together.

Tears welled in my eyes, but I blinked them back, determined to stay strong—for Levi, our children, and our grandchildren. The journey ahead was uncertain and daunting, but with faith, love, and the support of my family, I knew I could face whatever came my way.

As the minutes dragged on, the anxiety gnawed at me, each second feeling like an eternity. I whispered a prayer under my breath, asking for strength, courage, and the grace to accept whatever news the doctor would bring. Levi took a long breath, and I glanced up at him, seeing the same fear mirrored in his eyes, yet there was also unwavering determination and love.

In that moment, I knew that no matter what lay ahead, we would walk this path together, hand in hand, hearts bound by faith and love, relying on the only strength we knew to pull from... the Lord.

***

Read more about Ruth in the seventh book of *The Amish Women of Lawrence County Series.*
Ruth's Amish Words of Faith

Through their travels, two women learn to face their trials with grace and resilience, finding strength in their friendship and faith. Ruth's gentle Amish wisdom and Wilma's English zest for life create a beautiful balance, bringing out the best in each other. As they navigate the highs and lows of their health journey, they embark on a cross-country trip to discover that true friendship knows no boundaries and that love and laughter can light even the darkest paths no matter where they travel.

WHAT DID YOU THINK?

First of all, thank you for purchasing *The Amish Women of Lawrence County – Savannah's Amish Ties That Bind.* I hope you will enjoy all the books in this series.

You could have picked any number of books to read, but you chose this book, and for that, I am incredibly grateful. I hope it added value and quality to your everyday life. If so, it would be nice to share this book with your friends and family on social media.

If you enjoyed this book and found some benefit in reading it, I'd like to hear from you and hope that you could take some time to post a review on Amazon. Your feedback and support will help me improve my writing craft for future projects.

If you loved visiting Willow Springs, I invite you to sign up for my private email list, where you'll get to explore more of the characters of this Amish Community.

Sign up at https://dl.bookfunnel.com/v9wmnj7kve and download the novella that starts this series, *The Amish Women of Lawrence County.*

GLOSSARY

Pennsylvania Dutch "Deutsch" Words

Ausbund. Amish songbook.

bruder. Brother.

datt. Father or dad.

denki. Thank You.

doddi. Grandfather.

doddi haus. A small house next to the main house.

g'may. Community.

goot meiya. Good morning.

jah. Yes.

kapp. Covering or prayer cap.

kinner. Children.

mamm. Mother or mom.

grossmommi. Grandmother.

nee. No.

Ordnung. Order or set of rules the Amish follow.

schwester. Sister.

singeon. Singing/youth gathering.

The Amish are a religious group typically referred to as Pennsylvania Dutch, Pennsylvania Germans, or Pennsylvania Deutsch. They are descents of early German immigrants to Pennsylvania, and their beliefs center around living a conservative lifestyle. They arrived between the late 1600s and the early 1800s to escape religious persecutions in Europe. They first settled in Pennsylvania with the promise of religious freedom by William Penn. Most Pennsylvania Dutch still speak a variation of their original German language as well as English.

ABOUT THE AUTHOR

Tracy Fredrychowski's life closely mirrors the gentle, simple stories she crafts in her writing. With a passion for the simpler side of life, Tracy regularly shares tips on her website and blog at tracyfredrychowski.com

In northwestern Pennsylvania, Tracy grew up steeping in the virtues of country living. A pivotal moment in her life was the tragic murder of a young Amish woman in her community.

This event profoundly influenced her, compelling her to dedicate her writing to the peaceful lives of the Amish people. Tracy aims to inspire her readers through her stories to embrace a life centered around faith, family, and community.

For those intrigued by the Amish way of life, Tracy extends an invitation to connect with her on Facebook. On her page and group, she shares captivating Amish photography by her friend Jim Fisher and recipes, short stories, and glimpses into her cherished Amish community nestled deep in the heart of northwestern Pennsylvania's Amish County.

Facebook.com/tracyfredrychowskiauthor/

Facebook.com/groups/tracyfredrychowski/

Printed in Great Britain
by Amazon

47312851R00189